W9-CBM-224

Missing Girls

by

Lois Metzger

SCHOLASTIC INC.
New York Toronto London Auckland Sydney
Mexico City New Delhi Hong Kong

ISBN 0-439-14724-7

12 11 10 9 8 7 6 5 4 3 2 1   0 1 2 3 4 5/0

Printed in the U.S.A.   40

First Scholastic printing, February 2000

Set in Granjon

To my brother, Steve

ACKNOWLEDGMENTS

Many people helped enormously along the way. Special thanks to my wonderful editor, Sharyn November, and also to Regina Hayes, President and Publisher of Viking Children's Books, and to my agent, Susan Cohen at Writers House. Also I greatly appreciate a stay at the MacDowell Colony, where I started this book.

My uncle, William K. Stern, shared his extraordinary life experiences with me over lunch, once a week, for two years. Many of the stories in this book belong to him. A complete account of his war years has been videotaped by Survivors of the Shoah Visual History Foundation; this project, created by Steven Spielberg, is the world's largest multimedia archive of Holocaust survivor testimony.

My father, David Metzger, died while I was writing this book. I am grateful to him for all his help. My grandmother, Erna Stern, and my mother, Ilse Metzger, have been gone for many years and they are here, too.

Steve Metzger, my brother, was always part of this book. Thanks, too, to generous friends who read it and offered just the right advice: Joan Budne, Rita Campon, Claudia Cohen, Gail Paris, Janina Quint, Liz Rosenberg, Josephine Stott, Amy Tonsits, Alexa Witt, Judith Zimmer.

Thanks for everything to Tony and Jacob.

Contents

Missing Girls

Bus Stop

Chapter 1

Carrie Schmidt stood at the bus stop with her grandmother, flipping slowly through *Life* magazine. The sweltering heat made the pages sticky and limp. Right in the middle, an advertisement for hair dye caught her eye.

> *Can you just shampoo in* BORN BLONDE?
> *Of course.*
> *Isn't this 1967?*

No question about it, the Born Blonde girl was pretty. But she wasn't spectacular like the woman on the cover—Veruschka, the most famous model in the world, with thick dark blonde hair like a lion's mane. Carrie made sure to read every word of the article on Veruschka, who was a towering 6 feet 4 inches, 120 pounds, and "miraculously pleasant."

Wait a minute, Carrie thought. She's over a foot taller than me but weighs six pounds less!

In one picture, Veruschka held a dandelion between her lips, and the caption quoted her—*"They say I have the 'future look,' as if I'm looking beyond the camera into something else."*

"I know about that girl," Carrie's grandmother said, pointing at *Life*. "She's German. Her father did get killed—executed—for plotting to kill Hitler."

Carrie sighed. "Hitler is not a miraculously pleasant subject, you know."

"And why should we not discuss Hitler?" her grandmother said, sharp blue eyes on Carrie.

Carrie knew the look—*I talk, you listen, you talk, I listen. What's wrong with that?* "Because I'm hot, it's so hot," Carrie said. "Because I need a nap."

"Another one?"

Yes, she'd already taken a nap, after lunch, but it had somehow left her feeling more tired than before. "Because there must be other things to talk about while waiting for a bus." The sun was hazy, making the air slightly blurry, almost visible. She wiped sweat off her upper lip.

"Carrie, why do you wear long pants in such heat?"

"I don't like shorts."

"Why not? You'd be more comfortable."

Trust her grandmother to find a subject as bad as Hitler. Carrie always wore big shirts and long pants in dark colors, clothes to cover her up and make her invisible—though that wasn't always possible, since sometimes you could practically see the air. "Where's the bus, already?" she muttered.

"Carrie, it's not yet twenty minutes."

But even fifteen minutes in Belle Heights, Queens, felt like an hour anyplace else. Tomorrow would be the first day of school, almost three weeks late because of a teachers' strike. Carrie was going to be "the new kid." New to eighth grade, new to the school, new to Belle Heights, new to the guest room in her grandmother's house—where she'd be living for a year, while her father was in Las Vegas, handling publicity for boxers.

"Oh, look," her grandmother said, squinting at something beyond Carrie. "Here's that woman and her daughter I did tell you about."

"What woman? What daughter?"

"I did tell you. You don't listen."

"But I—"

"Mrs. Brockner, how nice," her grandmother said, as Carrie spun around and clamped her mouth shut.

The woman hesitated. "I'm sorry?"

"We spoke not last week at the A&P, Mrs. Brockner."

"Yes, of course," Mrs. Brockner said, not remembering any more than Carrie did. Carrie could tell. She watched Mrs. Brockner take in all of her grandmother, who practically wore a sign around her neck—IMMIGRANT. After twenty years in this country, she still had a thick accent that seemed to get even thicker around strangers. Carrie even called her "Mutti," the German word for "mommy"—it rhymed with "sooty." Just a bit taller than Carrie, she wore a rain bonnet tightly tied at her chin, squashing her cloud of white hair, and held a clear plastic umbrella that, when open, looked like the Liberty Bell. She had on thick brown shoes, a sleeveless, stretchy plaid top, baby blue slacks, and no jewelry.

Mrs. Brockner could have worn a sign of her own—AMERICAN. Carrie figured she was American all the way back to flappers and bootleggers. Of course Carrie was American, too, born and raised in Spruce Hills, Queens, four miles and three busses away from Belle Heights. But she didn't feel American. At the luncheonette where Mutti worked, Carrie had once tasted gazpacho. It was chillingly cold and crunchy, unlike "real soup" which was neither. Carrie felt about as American as gazpacho felt like soup.

Mrs. Brockner, on the other hand, was the real McCoy— sturdy, bouncy, comfortable inside her own skin. She wore shiny white sandals and a flowery pink-and-white baby-doll dress; her chin-length blonde hair curled behind dangling beaded earrings; she smelled wonderfully of lilacs, freshening even the muggy, polluted air of Belle Heights; and her perfect nails were polished cherry red.

Carrie tried to remember if her own mother had worn nail polish. If she had, what color? Four years after her mother's death, almost all Carrie had left was an impression—that her mother was tall and serene, with a core of happiness that made her seem lit from within, reminding Carrie of how, as a kid, she'd put a flashlight against her palm to see the red glow between her fingers. But with each year Carrie lost more details, as if her mother were an Etch-A-Sketch drawing slowly being turned over and shaken.

"You must call me Rochelle," Mrs. Brockner said. "And this is my daughter."

The daughter looked mad. That was what Carrie noticed first. As if someone had just said something to her and she sure didn't like it. She could be pretty, if she didn't look so mad. Thin, on the tall side, with smooth, pale skin, and hair that was long and dark and straight as thread. Carrie's hair was shorter and always frizzy, even more so on hot days. The daughter carried a small folded-up umbrella and wore plain white bermuda shorts and a sleeveless pale blue top—just clothes, nothing more. Carrie always made an effort to look like she didn't care what she had on. This girl really didn't care.

". . . Carrie, my granddaughter," Mutti was saying, gently pushing Carrie forward. "It's short for Carol. Such a pretty name, Carrie's mother always said, a song for a name."

"Carol is a perfectly charming name," Mrs. Brockner said. "You're the same age as my Mona, aren't you?"

"Thirteen," Carrie replied, thinking that *Mona* wasn't a particularly charming name. It had "moan" in it.

"Yes, you'll be in eighth grade together—tomorrow, thank heaven. I mean, teachers deserve the money, heaven knows, but wasn't this strike awful?"

"Yes and no," Mutti said—which was how she often answered questions. "Carrie did just move here, not three weeks ago. It did give Carrie a chance to settle down."

"We adore Belle Heights!" Mrs. Brockner opened her arms, embracing the street behind the bus stop—typical Belle Heights, with a curvy concrete sidewalk lined with brownish trees, a couple of plain shop fronts, a long row of semi-attached houses behind patches of lawn. "It's so calm and peaceful here, a pocket of quiet. No crime, no antiwar demonstrations, no riots . . ."

To Carrie, Belle Heights, out in the far reaches of an outer borough of New York City, also felt more like an absence than a presence, a nothing instead of a something. It wasn't quaint and friendly, like a small town. It wasn't thrilling, like the center of a big city. It wasn't hushed and beautiful, like the countryside. In fact, it looked washed-out, colorless—a smudge of a neighborhood.

"She's German," Mona said, pointing at Veruschka.

Mrs. Brockner laughed. "So what, darling? Maybe this nice lady is German, too."

"Born in Austria," Mutti said. "Do you now"—which was how Mutti sometimes said "Do you know"—"that Veruschka's father did get killed for trying to kill Hitler?"

"Yes," Mona said. "He was part of a whole group that tried and failed. They came awfully close."

"What can you do?" Mutti smiled sadly. "You can nothing do."

Carrie winced. Why did Mutti have to talk backward like that? How was Carrie ever going to get through life without her mother and with somebody like Mutti?

"Oh, look!" Mrs. Brockner cried out. "Carol's got the most adorable dimple, right there."

Carrie couldn't believe it. No one, not even Mutti or her two best friends back home, had ever noticed that dimple, a tiny line between her chin and right cheek. No one, that is, except for Carrie's mother—who also called her *Carol* even after everyone else had switched to *Carrie*. "No one ever notices it," Carrie said.

"You should wear your hair back, so it's easier to see." Mrs. Brockner stared hard at Carrie. "You have a lovely shape to your face, and completely acceptable features, but your hair just sticks out, and those bangs don't suit you—"

Mona said, *"Mother."*

"Well, it's true. Carol doesn't mind a few personal remarks, do you, Carol?"

"No." Carrie looked directly at Mona. She figured Mona would get even madder, but the expression in her large blue eyes had changed. Somehow, Mona, too, had that look. The Future Look.

"Of course," Mrs. Brockner said, "we can't all have hair like Veruschka's."

"Her hair's amazing!" Carrie said. "It's like a lion's mane."

"Why, yes, that's true!" Mrs. Brockner smiled at Carrie, who felt warm all over—not in a bad, sweaty way, either.

"I see you also did bring an umbrella," Mutti said to Mona.

"You never know." Mona shrugged. "It's been raining all summer."

"I thought it was the Summer of Love, not the Summer of Rain." Mrs. Brockner winked at Carrie.

For Carrie, it had been the Summer of Busses—visiting her best friends in Spruce Hills, Lolly and Trippy. Days with them just slipped by so comfortably—braiding Lolly's waist-length hair, eating Yankee Doodles, making fun of shows on TV while carefully watching them, anyway. But it felt strange, too, knowing that in the same big building a whole other family was living in the Schmidts' apartment—a mother, a father, and two boys. It was only for a year, but still.

"And now, we really must go," Mrs. Brockner said, with her pleasant smile. She placed a hand on Mona's shoulder, who flinched. "Relatives coming for dinner, you understand."

"Oh, yes." Mutti nodded. "We're going downtown, to buy

Carrie some closes for school." *Clothes*, Carrie wanted to explain to Mrs. Brockner, who looked a little confused. More big shirts, more long pants—more darker darks, if that was possible. "Downtown" meant the heart of Belle Heights, not faraway Manhattan—where Carrie went by subway maybe once a year, to see a show at Rockefeller Center.

"Nice to see you again, Mrs. Brockner," Mutti said. Carrie wanted to nudge her. Mrs. Brockner had insisted on *Rochelle*. Now that was a charming name. Kind of French. "Nice to meet you, Mona."

Mona took a step forward and shook Mutti's hand. "Nice to meet you, too." She sounded like she actually meant it. Then she shook Carrie's hand, without a word. Carrie noticed that Mona was a terrible nail biter, fingertips red and raw, but her hand actually felt cool on this hot, muggy day.

As Mrs. Brockner and her daughter walked away, three busses screeched toward Carrie and Mutti. It always happened like that—you waited and waited, and then they all came at once, like locusts, or tests, or cliques. But two of the busses rattled by, as if going to a party Mutti and Carrie hadn't been invited to; only the most crowded one stopped.

"So, what did you think of her?" Mutti asked, looking up at Carrie. She had a seat because a barefoot guy with a ponytail had instantly stood up for her.

"She's great." Carrie strained to grab the rail high over her head. Veruschka could have reached it, easy. But Carrie couldn't picture Veruschka on a Belle Heights bus. "I liked her nails."

Mutti paused. "I did mean the daughter."

The bus lurched, groaned, shuddered. Belle Boulevard was a

10

busy, two-way street, hilly as a roller coaster, and they were on a tight curve. "She's all right," Carrie said.

"I did like her. Very much."

"You mean—Mona?"

"I mean Mona."

Chapter 2

Back home at the square metal table in her tiny, dark kitchen, Mutti opened a "blue letter." That was what Carrie called it, an airmail letter from abroad, a single long piece of blue tissue-like paper that, folded over, became its own envelope and was so thin it looked like it could melt in your hands. Mutti opened it carefully, with a knife.

"Carrie!" Mutti said, delighted. "Angus Fraser does want to come!"

The name sounded familiar but Carrie couldn't place it. Ever since her mother died, Carrie felt she had the memory of a fly. Which was to say, no memory at all. Flies will land on the same hot surface over and over, forgetting every time what happened before. "That's nice," Carrie said, not sure if it was nice or not.

Mutti eyed Carrie. "You don't remember who he is."

"Sure I do! He's—he's somebody who lives far away."

"Carrie, he did take care of your mother during the war. She did live on his farm in Scotland, where she was safe."

Carrie thought hard for a moment. Angus Fraser, Angus Fraser, Angus Fraser. Her mother had adored him, that fact came back. More like a feeling than a fact. And he'd visited once before, when Carrie was about five and her mother was sparkling with life and health. Carrie was sparkling, too—a little thing who jumped around people like a puppy. Would Angus Fraser remember that? What did she remember about him? That he had a big grin, like the one the Cheshire Cat left behind. "Why is he coming? Who invited him?"

"Nobody. He's always had a stand-up invitation."

"*Standing* invitation," Carrie corrected her.

"Yes, a standing invitation. He picked November to come stand."

It should be something to look forward to, a visit from Angus Fraser, but it wasn't. Carrie felt the pit inside her, where her insides should be, the pit that had opened up when her mother died. November—how far away was that? She got lost in time. Was it February now? No, way too hot for February. July? No—September. Almost October. And October was right next to November. Soon, too soon . . . She stood and opened Mutti's tiny freezer, which needed defrosting, and pulled out a banana cake.

"We're having dinner soon," Mutti warned.

"I'll help, don't worry." They'd worked out a system—Mutti cooked, and Carrie did everything around the cooking. Setting up, clearing away, washing the dishes. Weekends she defrosted the freezer and vacuumed, too. Mutti did the laundry in the basement. Carrie had been down there only once. Strange—though she lived here now, there were parts of the house she hadn't even seen.

"I'm thinking of your appetite," Mutti said.

"I never lose my appetite."

Mutti went off to watch the six o'clock news. "I'll leave the letter on the table for you."

Carrie sat in the hazy darkness, staring at the letter. *My dear Hilde,* it began. Carrie remembered how shocked she'd been as a kid, seeing the name "Hilde Altmann" on Mutti's mail, positive the mailman had made a mistake. She was Mutti; she'd always been Mutti. Carrie didn't read any further. Instead, she cut a single sliver of banana cake with a knife, as delicate as a blue letter. And then a second sliver, also paper thin. As she ate, losing count of the slivers, she thought about the pit. Funny how she could eat and eat and still the pit was there. She remembered an Edgar Allan Poe story she'd read in English last year—"The Pit and the Pendulum." A man was strapped to a piece of wood and, high over his head, a razor-sharp pendulum swung in a huge arc. To his horror, he realized the pendulum was descending slowly. He spent days like that, watching the pendulum come closer and closer, knowing that eventually he would be sliced open.

Carrie thought—knowing it was as melodramatic as anything in an Edgar Allan Poe story—*I am in the pit. Angus Fraser is the pendulum.*

Carrie's father phoned during dinner. He called every night, or almost.

"Who's fighting tonight?" Carrie asked him.

"Vito the Invincible." Probably a name her father had come up with himself. "School start yet?"

"Tomorrow." This was about as long as their conversations got. Back before Carrie's mother died, he'd talked all the time, at home and on the subway, taking her to the city to see the fights. What she remembered most about them was how much boxers sweat, rivers of it down their necks and backs. Afterward, her father, never one to need much sleep, would stay up all night, typing press releases, and then talk to Carrie over breakfast. She knew all the many different levels of championships and what weight you had to be to achieve them (100 pounds, for example, was a junior flyweight; 147 pounds was a welterweight; over 185 was a heavyweight—Carrie, at 126, could be the female featherweight champion of the world). But when Carrie's mother died, her father had gotten lost in a dark cloud of silence. One night she'd asked him, was it true you met Mom on a bus? No, he'd answered, almost angrily, nothing like that. These days her father maybe wasn't so angry, but they still answered each other's questions as if they were sending telegrams and had to pay for each word.

Carrie was about to hang up, but something pushed her to add, "Angus Fraser is coming in November."

"No kidding!" He sounded surprised, pleased. "I'll come back for that." It seemed he might actually say more, but then only asked, "Let me know the date, okay?"

"Okay."

"See you—see you in the future, I guess."

That sounded funny. After all, you couldn't see somebody in the past, right?

Carrie's room was on the second floor of Mutti's house and faced curvy, tree-lined Belle Heights Road. From her window she could see, through waving branches, a row of attached brick houses identical to Mutti's, ghostly in the bluish streetlights. *This is my room now,* Carrie told herself, trying to feel at home in the dusty guest room which had stored old papers before it stored Carrie, and still smelled a little dry and tired. No mirror—but that was okay. She didn't like mirrors, your own face staring back as if expecting you to do something. She ran her fingers over the stiff, heavy, maroon bedspread, and gazed up at the beige walls, round ceiling light, burgundy curtains, and the only painting—the sun hanging low over an unknown ocean. You couldn't tell if you were facing east or west, if it was early morning or late afternoon, if the sun was rising or setting.

This room doesn't belong to a real American girl, Carrie thought. It's an immigrant's room.

She could go downstairs to call Lolly or Trippy. But what was there to say? It's hot and I'm tired, yeah, yeah, I know I always say that, and I'll be starting my new school tomorrow, with a bunch of total strangers, strangers who aren't strangers to each other, of course, they've been in school together, most of them, since kindergarten . . . and, oh, yeah, this guy is visiting soon—no, not that kind of guy (Carrie could hear Lolly so easily assuming that Angus Fraser was cute and young), he's old, he took care of my mother years and years ago, and no, I don't want to see him, no, it isn't sweet, no, like I said, *I don't want to see him,* no, don't ask me because I don't know why, or maybe it's because I was jumping around and he had a big grin, I just don't know, I wish I did, I only know I don't want to see him. . . .

Mutti had bought her a diary just before she moved in. The pages were still blank, and the key didn't work right, it kept bending. Now, suddenly, Carrie picked it up. A weird thought came into her head. What if this belonged to the girl she'd met today? Mrs. Brockner's daughter—Mona. What would Mona Brockner say?

Dear Diary, Carrie wrote, changing her regular handwriting—less slanted, more up-and-down. *My name is Mona Brockner. I'm mad. I don't know why. Or maybe I do know why and I'm just not telling you.* That sounded like it could be Mona Brockner. *I'm pretty, only I don't care. I'm probably the only girl in Belle Heights who doesn't care about such a thing. Or maybe I don't know I'm pretty. I'm not sure.* This was getting confusing. *But if you pin me down, I'd say that on a scale from 1 to 100, I'm a 90. Veruschka's a 96 and Carrie Schmidt's a 32.* That sounded about right. *My mother's an 85. She's not as pretty as me, her eyes are too close together.* Carrie hadn't noticed that until now. *Carrie's mother, on the other hand, was a 99.*

Carrie stopped writing. Mona had no way of knowing that.

Chapter 3

It rained as Carrie walked to school. Belle Heights Junior High, J.H.S. 207. Funny, her old school had been J.H.S. 206. This made her sound one step closer to . . . what?

Carrie wore her new navy blue button-down long sleeved shirt, and it clung to her back; her legs rubbed together in new black pants; her umbrella had a couple of broken spokes—still, it kept the rain off. She'd slept her usual ten hours, but could have slept another ten. Carrie loved to sleep. Sometimes she tried to catch the moment she actually went from *awake* to *asleep,* but it was too blurry. Sometimes going from *asleep* to *awake* felt blurry, too—but that blur stayed with her.

Wake up! she ordered herself. *First day! New school!*

Belle Heights Junior High could have been the identical twin of Spruce Hills Junior High. Brick box for about a thousand kids, concrete playground with no trees, greenish fluorescent lights. It felt more crowded here, or maybe that was because all the faces were unfamiliar. The girls looked older. Some wore thigh-high skirts over fishnet stockings; others, in hip-hugging pants and halter tops, displayed a lot more skin than Carrie ever dared to show.

Carrie found her homeroom on a list near the front door, and sat at one of the big wooden desks with a drawer underneath, near a window overlooking the playground. That girl Mona Brockner was in some other homeroom. Carrie listened to all the kids catching up with each other. *Wasn't the strike great? Yeah, long summer! . . . Did you see Gina's nose? She went to that doctor, the one downtown—yeah, the same one who did Liz and Tina—can you believe it, now they all have the same nose! . . . That Craig Forrest is cuter than ever—we broke up before the summer, but maybe now we can get back together. . . .*

Two girls sat in front of Carrie. One wore a gauzy white peasant dress, practically to the floor, and had beautiful brown hair that fell in delicate curls around her face; the other was in gray, with long black hair parted in the middle and thick black eyeliner around dark eyes. They whispered nonstop until the bell rang loudly at eight-thirty.

A tall woman with orange hair entered the room and wrote her name in bold chalk on the blackboard: MRS. MENDOZA. Some kids groaned. Did she have a reputation? "I must have quiet," she said. "We will take attendance—*shhh!*"

Someone had maybe coughed a little. Clearly Mrs. Mendoza took this silence business very seriously.

"I am your homeroom teacher. When I call your name, you will say, 'Present.' I do not wish to hear clever variations. Do not get on my nerves in homeroom because I will be grading many of you in Geology, Biology, and Math. New math, I should say. Time to forget all about the old math." Carrie could feel the nervousness in the room, but she relaxed. Those were good subjects for her, especially math—old or new, it didn't matter. Her

19

worst subject was history. She barely passed it last year. She couldn't hold dates in her head; she never knew what followed what.

Mrs. Mendoza called out names and passed out schedule cards; when she said, "Carol Schmidt," Carrie called out, "Present!" Several boys turned to look at Carrie, and then turned away, not interested. It didn't bother her. As far as she was concerned, boys were from another planet. They had their mail forwarded to earth.

But the girl with the curls whipped around. "You're new." It sounded like a challenge.

Carrie nodded.

"No talking!" Mrs. Mendoza snapped. "I must have quiet!"

The girl faced forward. Her name, it turned out, was Regina Gold. Her friend was June Zucker.

At one point Mrs. Mendoza called out, "Ruby Stevens"—but there was no Ruby Stevens. "Does anyone know where Ruby might be?" Mrs. Mendoza asked.

Regina raised her hand. "I think she ran away. She's in the East Village somewhere—she's a missing girl." Several kids laughed. Maybe they knew Regina and knew she was making this up.

"It's not amusing," Mrs. Mendoza said sharply. "If it's true, it's a very sad thing, a tragedy. These are children who leave the safety of their parents' homes and run away, most likely into terrible danger. You will remain quiet, until we finish attendance."

They all sat in tomblike silence—which only made them more aware of every smothered laugh, every rustle of paper. Carrie got a strange feeling. *I'm a missing girl.* She heard it echo in her head without ever having said it. *I'm a missing girl.* But I'm not, she told herself firmly. I'm right here, how could I be a missing girl? *I'm a missing girl.* The first period bell rang, shattering Mrs. Mendoza's silence.

Regina and June and nearly everyone else got up and left. Carrie looked at her schedule and stayed exactly where she was. Her first class, it turned out, was Geology with Mrs. Mendoza.

Over the next half hour, Carrie learned why Belle Heights was a bus driver's nightmare—and, she had to admit, it was interesting. Over the last million years, the earth had alternated between warming and cooling. Each new ice age, glaciers—sheets of ice a thousand feet thick, as tall as the Empire State Building—moved slowly south and then north again. As it moved, a glacier scraped up tons of rock, sand, and clay, and pushed it on ahead of itself. When the glacier went back up north, it left all the rock, sand, and clay behind. "This rocky ridge is called the terminal moraine," Mrs. Mendoza said. "And Belle Heights is built right on top of it."

"So Belle Heights is the garbage dump of the Ice Age," one kid called out, and Mrs. Mendoza didn't disagree, though she did remind him to raise his hand before speaking. Just before the bell, she announced, "Class, start thinking now about an end-of-the-year project. The theme is—'The Earth Is Our Home.'"

"It isn't mine," somebody cracked, and kids laughed.

Carrie didn't see why that was funny.

In the cafeteria, Carrie sipped milk and ate macaroni and cheese as orange as Mrs. Mendoza's hair. She'd taken two dishes of Jell-O for dessert—one red, one green. Like traffic lights.

21

"Where are you from?" Carrie heard over her shoulder, more like a demand than a question, as Regina sat down next to her.

"Spruce Hills," Carrie said.

"Never heard of it." Regina sounded suspicious, as if Carrie had invented an entirely new neighborhood.

"I have," June said quietly, sitting on Carrie's other side. Now Carrie felt like a book between bookends. June had on a fuzzy pale gray sweater and was rubbing her arms briskly. It had gotten cooler but Carrie was still hot. "It's pretty far away, right?"

"Right. Four miles, three busses. That sweater's nice. What is it, mohair?"

June nodded. "It's Regina's."

"I hate busses," Regina said. "I get carsick. Or bus sick."

"You're living in the wrong place," Carrie told her. "Belle Heights is the bus capital of the world."

"I hate Belle Heights," Regina said. "It's so boring. You ever smoke pot, Carol?"

"Actually, it's Carrie, everyone calls me Carrie." She stalled a moment. Drugs, like boys, weren't really her thing. Come to think of it, nothing was really her thing, except maybe sleeping or eating.

"You ever smoke pot, *Carrie?*" Regina said.

Carrie shook her head.

"Neither have we," Regina said. "But one time I was on a bus when kids were smoking and I took a really deep breath."

"Maybe that's why you got bus sick."

"No, that was only the one time. You know any kids here in Belle Heights, Carrie?"

"Only you two." Just then, across the entire noisy cafeteria, she spotted Mona Brockner, sitting by herself.

"Really," Regina said, challenging again.

"Let's look at our schedules and see if we overlap," June said.

They didn't, except in homeroom, and Regina and June only had French and Cooking together. Suddenly June cried out, "Oh, my God! This is awful! Speech class!"

"What's the big deal?" Regina said. "You just get up and talk. Besides, you can't do any worse than Mona Brockner did last year."

"Mona Brockner?" Carrie said. "How do you know Mona Brockner?"

Regina squinted at her. "The question is, how do *you* know her? I thought you didn't know anyone."

"I just remembered. I met her yesterday at the bus stop."

"Who else did you meet at the bus stop?"

"No one." With Regina, everything was like a test. Somehow June had been given a passing grade. "Why did Mona give such a bad speech?"

"It wasn't really her fault," June said. "She just didn't explain her subject very well—"

"She's crazy," Regina said. "There's a padded room, waiting for her. She said you could be asleep and awake at the same time. Crazy, right? Like seeing UFOs. Everybody laughed. Even the teacher couldn't help it."

June cleared her throat. "It was more like this, I think—that sometimes while you're asleep and dreaming you can realize you're dreaming, so you're kind of awake, too, at least to that."

Carrie sat there a moment, absorbing this. Dreams were, just

23

by themselves, interesting—the dream sequence in a movie always held Carrie's attention. *Alice's Adventures in Wonderland,* her favorite book, was the story of a dream. Her favorite old song, "Sh-boom," had that great line, "Life could be a dream." But this struck Carrie as more than just "interesting." She wanted to talk to Mona, find out about being awake while asleep; she felt a rush inside her, as if she had to hurry up and get somewhere.

"You shouldn't eat that." Regina pointed at Carrie's Jell-O. "Chemicals galore."

But Carrie liked Jell-O. She'd already finished the green, and was looking forward to the red.

"Regina always tells me what to eat and what not to eat." June sounded pleased. "Sometimes she brings fresh fruit."

"Why is Mona so strange?" Carrie asked.

"She wasn't always that way," June said. "She used to be so—"

"Not anymore," Regina cut her off. "Look, there's Craig Forrest! Would you die if he asked you out?"

Carrie looked at Craig Forrest. Not bad. Tall, big shoulders, carrot red hair. "I wouldn't die," Carrie said, "but I might get bus sick."

June laughed.

"Really," Regina said, removing the red Jell-O.

At the end of the day, Regina invited Carrie over.

There was no door to her room, just a beaded curtain that clacked when you went in or out. No chairs, just big bright pillows, a fluffy white shag rug, a mattress on the floor, piles of clothes, and posters everywhere—Simon and Garfunkel, a black-and-white spiral that made you dizzy just to look at it, cute kittens all in a heap. The pillows, Carrie realized when she leaned back on one, looked soft but were actually as unyielding as glaciers. Regina and June stacked up forty-fives for the record player, and Carrie played with Dinah, Regina's calico cat.

"Dinah," Carrie said. "That's Alice's cat in *Alice in Wonderland*. Is that your favorite book, too?"

"She's not Alice's cat," Regina said. "She's Dinah as in, 'Someone's in the kitchen with.' "

"Oh," Carrie was disappointed. It's only the name of the cat, she told herself, but she couldn't shake the feeling.

Regina's mother looked older than Mrs. Brockner—though not as old as Mutti, of course. She had short gray hair and round glasses, and wore an apron that said, "The Chef Accepts Compliments." After she offered them chocolate chip cookies, which Regina refused on their behalf, they didn't see Mrs. Gold again.

"She makes me sick!" Regina said. "Women can be anything now, and she's just a housewife! I *hate* her!"

"I like your mother," June said. "She's always been so nice to me. I don't think my mother even knows my name—"

"She's so nice to everybody! It doesn't mean anything! It makes me sick!" From one of her piles, Regina pulled out a cardigan sweater that looked like a black caterpillar—with a few orange-and-white cat hairs on it. "My mom gave me this for my birthday. Feel, Carrie."

Carrie rubbed the sleeve between her fingers. "Soft," she said.

"It's my favorite. Cashmere. Want to borrow it? Go on, try

it." Now there wasn't a hint of disgust. Carrie, slipping on the exquisitely soft sweater, knew that Regina didn't really hate her mother. It was just something you were supposed to say.

Mutti and Carrie watched the six o'clock news. Mutti did this every night, without fail, and watched the news at eleven, too, and read *The New York Times* cover to cover, including the column of VIETNAM WAR DEAD FROM THIS AREA. Mutti had been through World War II already. Wasn't that enough?

They sat on Mutti's yellow couch, facing a tall bookcase with books on the top and bottom and a black-and-white TV in the middle. It was dark except for the inky blue light of the TV. Mutti was soaking her feet in warm water and Epsom salts, something she did sometimes. And Carrie again heard that echo in her head. *I'm a missing girl.*

"How was the first day of school?" Mutti asked.

"Fine. I made three friends. No, wait a minute." Carrie could feel herself frown. "Two."

"This is good."

The phone in the kitchen rang, and Carrie went to answer it.

"Carrie, how was school?" Her father.

"Fine. I made two friends. How was Vito the Invincible?"

"Vincible," he answered wearily.

When Carrie got back to the living room, Mutti was crying. On TV, the bodies of American soldiers in Vietnam were being loaded onto helicopters. "Mutti, if it makes you cry, how can you watch?"

"How can I not?"

✳   ✳   ✳

26

Over the weekend Carrie visited Lolly and Trippy back in Spruce Hills, where if you didn't live in a tall, brick apartment building, you lived in a short, brick apartment building. They watched hours and hours of TV, played Monopoly, and even brought out old Barbie dolls. Lolly and Trippy played with Carrie the way they always had. So why, in the middle of it, did Carrie wonder what she was doing with girls who used baby names? Lolly was Lorraine and Trippy was Margaret. Come on!

Taking three busses out of the old neighborhood made Carrie feel . . . stale. She'd seen a sign in a bakery that could have described her: DAY-OLD BREAD. It was cheaper than bread fresh out of the oven.

Sunday night, Carrie dreamed. It was a dream she'd had for four years now, and it always tricked her. She wondered, after, why she never knew it was just a dream.

There was Carrie's mother—in black and white, which turned her red hair dark and her green eyes to gray. She wouldn't look at Carrie or talk to Carrie. She didn't seem like herself—too sad, troubled. But Carrie was happy, so happy to see her, so happy she might explode! All that stuff—getting sick and dying—had been a mistake, a big mistake, so big you could laugh about it. In fact, Carrie laughed in the dream, laughed until her stomach hurt.

Waking up, and remembering, Carrie always felt like wreckage.

But this time she remembered, too, about Mona Brockner and how you could wake up inside your dreams.

27

Chapter 4

In homeroom Monday morning, Ruby Stevens showed up. She hadn't been a missing girl, after all—she'd had chicken pox. Mrs. Mendoza, after taking attendance, said she would allow "gentle whispers."

Regina turned around and stuck out her arm. "Feel, Carrie."

Carrie, wearing the black caterpillar cardigan, touched Regina's extra thick, off-white sweater. "Soft," she said, again.

"Regina's mother just got it for her." June turned around, too. "Regina said I could wear it."

"I couldn't. I'd bake like a meatloaf." That wasn't what Carrie had planned to say—she'd meant to invite them over to Mutti's house that afternoon. When she did finally ask, and they said yes, she got to the hard part. Lifting her voice up a notch to sound light and carefree, she said, "And Mona Brockner, too, okay?"

Regina almost fell off her chair. "Are you *serious*? Are you seriously serious?"

"Gentle whispers," Mrs. Mendoza reminded her.

"It might be fun," Carrie said with a shrug, as if she didn't care one way or the other, "learning about dreams and stuff."

"It's nice," June said quietly. "I think you're a nice person, Carrie."

But Carrie didn't feel particularly nice. She wasn't so nice to Mutti. And not wanting to see Angus Fraser again certainly wasn't nice. Anyway, Carrie wanted to be beyond nice. She wanted to be . . . miraculously pleasant.

"I don't believe this," Regina said. "Mona Brockner."

"I'm sure if Mona is really too weird, we won't ask her again. Right, Carrie?" June raised her eyebrows.

"Right." Carrie noticed that they had become a "we." Regina and June were now her Belle Heights Lolly and Trippy. Carrie tried to feel all cozy and settled in, like a marshmallow in cocoa, the way she used to feel in Spruce Hills. But it might take some time.

All through Math that morning, Carrie wondered how she would actually get Mona Brockner to come over. Mona wasn't exactly friendly. There was a surprise pop quiz; Carrie got nine out of ten answers right. Now she had to get the right answer out of Mona.

When Carrie saw Mona by herself in the cafeteria, she almost couldn't do it. But she remembered that it was October now, and next month was November, and the pendulum was swinging. This thing with Mona and the dreams—it didn't exactly keep the pendulum away, but it somehow kept Carrie from having to stare up at it. Angus Fraser could simply be an old man who lived far away and had nothing to do with her.

"We met at the bus stop," Carrie said, leaning on one of the empty chairs across from Mona. "Remember?"

"I remember."

"A couple of kids are coming to my house today. Want to hang out with us?"

Mona didn't answer right away. Then she said, "Who? Who's coming over?"

A girl like that, alone all the time—you'd think she'd jump at the chance. "Does it matter?"

Mona nodded.

Carrie pointed out Regina and June. Mona got quiet again, before asking, "Why do you want me to come?"

This was even harder than Carrie had imagined. "Because the end-of-the-year project in Mrs. Mendoza's class is 'My Home Is Your Home' and you're my homework, okay?"

Mona stared at her.

"It's a joke," Carrie said.

"I know. I have Mrs. Mendoza third period. It's 'The Earth Is Our Home.' "

Carrie stared back at her.

"I can come, but I'll have to call my mother and get her permission."

That sounded so old-fashioned, especially when Mona's mother looked so hip. "You can call from my house. I have a phone. Actually I have running water and electricity, too."

Mona didn't say a word.

"It's another joke," Carrie said.

"I know."

Carrie sighed. "We'll meet in front of the school at three, okay?"

Mona nodded.

* * *

At three o'clock Mona stood at the school entrance, as neutral as if waiting for a bus. "It's so nice and bright out," Carrie said awkwardly, while walking with her to Mutti's house. Regina and June were several paces behind them. "Not like last week, right? Not like the Summer of Rain. Not today, not a cloud in sight, nothing!"

Mona barely said a word.

Most weekdays Mutti worked at her luncheonette until late afternoon, getting ready for the next day's breakfasts and lunches. The place was actually called "Luncheonette," as if it wore a sign around its neck.

Once they got to the house, Regina and June sat on one section of the couch, while Carrie pulled back the curtains and turned on two standing lamps. It didn't help much. The room looked like night, twenty-four hours a day.

Mona looked around. "The phone?"

"In here." Carrie led her to the kitchen. It was dark in there, too—Carrie wondered if she should give everybody miners' helmets with little lamps in the front. She took a six-pack of Coke from the refrigerator and, from a high shelf, a package of Vienna Fingers.

"Nothing for me, thanks," Mona said. "I'll just have running water."

"What?"

Mona remained as expressionless as Mount Rushmore. "You told me you had electricity and running water. Remember?"

It took Carrie a moment to realize that Mona was joking, too.

From Mutti's squat, black phone, Mona dialed a number. "Mrs. Brockner, please. This is her daughter."

31

Mona must be calling her mother at work, only it hadn't happened too often, or wouldn't the other person know Mona's voice? Carrie straightened out a dishtowel on a rack.

"Hello, I'm at Carrie's house. Carrie, the girl at the bus stop. *Carol*. The one with the grand—yes, that one."

Of course Mrs. Brockner remembers me, Carrie thought. She straightened out the same towel again.

"Well, I'm very sorry I interrupted you but I'm not home and you always said that I have to call—well, how am I supposed to know when the rules suddenly change?" Mona didn't sound too sorry. There was the anger again, fiery hot. "I'll get everything done after five, I promise." Homework? "No. No. No. No." What was Mrs. Brockner asking her, anyway? Mona just hung up without saying good-bye. What a shame, Carrie thought. If Carrie were Mrs. Brockner's daughter, she'd say, " 'Bye, Mom! Love you!"

"I have to be home by five," Mona said, no trace of the anger now.

"I heard. Do you like Vienna Fingers?"

Mona shrugged.

"I love to eat. It's my favorite thing, next to sleeping. I love how food tastes, I love swallowing, I love how food feels going down, how you get nice and warm and full." Why on earth was she telling Mona this?

"Food is just . . . food. It, you know, keeps you going, so you don't starve."

"It's more than that. But the trouble is—" And Carrie looked down at herself.

"You look just fine," Mona said, kindly.

32

"Hey!" Regina called from the living room. "Anybody home in there?"

Mona and Carrie looked at each other a moment. Regina sounded like Mrs. Mendoza. They almost smiled at each other.

Back in the living room, Carrie pulled the ring off a Coke can, took a deep swallow, and said something about her grandmother working so they had the place to themselves.

"How nice," June said, "that your grandmother lives with you."

"My grandmother lives at my house, too," Mona said.

"She does?" Carrie didn't think they had too much in common, except maybe boring clothes.

"Off and on," Mona said, and paused. "Mostly on."

Regina rolled her eyes.

"Was she a flapper?" Carrie asked.

Mona frowned. "Just a housewife. Until her husband died. Are you still a housewife if your husband is dead?"

Carrie cleared her throat. "Actually, it's not exactly that my grandmother lives with me. I live with her. This is my grandmother's house. See, my mother died."

June put her hand to her mouth. "Oh, my God, Carrie! How sad. Did she just die?"

"Four years ago. I lived with my father in Spruce Hills. My grandmother came over a lot, but it was hard for her, with all the busses and everything. Then my father got a job in Las Vegas for a year, and that's why I'm here."

"You're only here for a year?" Mona said.

Carrie nodded.

"It's still so sad," June said.

The whole first year after Carrie's mother died, she hadn't even known whether she should mention it to people or not. One time she blurted it out, and a kid said back, "So we all got problems, okay?" Mutti told her later that a dead parent is so scary, some kids can't bear to be reminded it might happen. It was easier, Mutti said, to think that by snubbing Carrie they were making themselves safe. So Carrie had to learn how to guess who'd make her feel better or worse—when was the right time or the wrong time. Now she had a pretty good idea. But it was always a risk.

"There are worse things than a mother who dies," Mona said.

Carrie wondered if this had been a wrong time, after all.

"What's that supposed to mean?" Regina said. "When your father dies, too?"

"No," Mona said. "When your mother . . . when she makes you feel a certain way, when she behaves a certain way, when certain things happen . . . well, it could be worse, is all I'm saying."

Carrie could see Mona ruining a speech about dreams. When she got nervous, words got all mixed up in her mouth.

"Is that your mother?" June pointed to the only framed photograph in the room, a slightly faded one, up on top of the bookcase. Carrie nodded. "How old is she there? She looks so young."

In the picture, it looked as if Carrie's mother wasn't sure whether to smile. "I don't know. Nineteen, maybe."

"No," Mona said, "you're wrong. She's our age."

"Thirteen? Not even close."

"The shape of the face is yours."

34

"Well, of course you can't see it, because it's black and white, but she had red hair and green eyes—"

"You look a lot like her," Mona said.

"She was very beautiful," Carrie added, with emphasis.

Mona nodded. "Yes, she was."

Carrie figured that weird Mona had gotten everything all mixed up. Or maybe there never was a right time to talk about it.

"I can't eat this." Regina frowned at the cookies and Coke. "Dreams, didn't you want to ask Mona about her dreams?"

"What for?" Mona straightened her shoulders.

"No, not your dreams, not exactly." Carrie wished she understood just what it was she wanted from Mona. "I want to know how to—I mean, is it something you could learn? You know, being awake while you're dreaming."

"You mean lucid dreaming?" Mona asked.

"Yes, exactly," Carrie said, though she'd never heard of it before. But it sounded right, and so beautiful, like skating on a frozen-over pond in moonlight.

"You're awake while you're dreaming," Mona said. "You know you're dreaming while you're dreaming. It's for real. I've done it."

Carrie felt a charge inside, like hooking up a wire in a science experiment and getting tiny lights to flash on and buzzers to buzz.

"Last year you made it sound like you could wake up and be in a dream world or something," June said. "You're saying it a little better now."

"I was so nervous then!"

"Can you teach us?" Carrie tried to sound casual.

"Yes, can you?" June was all excitement.

"I can try." Mona shrugged. "I mean, I learned from my mother—in a way. She went to a bunch of lectures last year on lucid dreaming, and told us all about it at dinner. Sometimes when she talks, it's stupid and boring. Sometimes it's actually interesting." Mrs. Brockner had looked to Carrie as if anything she touched would turn to interesting—a sort of Queen Midas. "This year it's analysis through hypnosis. Next year, who knows?"

"My mother's a lawyer," June said. "She never tells me anything."

"I can't stand it!" Regina sighed loudly. "Am I the only one here with a mother who does absolutely nothing?"

There was a silence. Carrie remembered, just then, that her mother had done volunteer work in the community—she could see her sitting by the phone, perfect posture, a take-charge person, so bright and upbeat and efficient, you'd never know that her thirtieth phone call wasn't her first. "My mother helped clean up Spruce Hills Park," Carrie said. "She made calls and arranged meetings and stuff."

"I can't stand it!" Regina said again. "Carrie's mother is *dead* and she did more than mine!"

Carrie cleared away the cookies and Coke (only she and Mona had eaten anything), and as soon as she got back from the kitchen, they began.

"You know," Mona said, "how when you're dreaming, you

sometimes think, *Am I dreaming?* Well, you never ask that question when you're awake, right?"

Wrong, thought Carrie. When her mother got sick, when her mother died, she'd asked it all the time. But now she just sat there and nodded.

"So if you're asking yourself if you're dreaming, then you *are* dreaming. Try to remember that. The problem is, dreams feel so real. They feel as real as . . . real life. But there are mistakes inside every dream. Things that tip you off."

"But—but—" Carrie let it hang there a moment. What if the dream felt real but the whole thing was a mistake, like when her mother appeared—alive, unsmiling, remote? "Dreams can be full of mistakes" was what Carrie ended up saying. "They're like jigsaw puzzles with pieces in all the wrong shapes."

Mona nodded. "That's why you have to know what to look for. And you have to know that you're looking." Regina's eyes started to glaze over. "There's a trick. In a dream, look at something in writing, anything—a book, a sign, a letter. Read the words, and then look away, and then read them again. The writing will always be different. If you see 'Three Blind Mice,' it could change to 'The Three Musketeers.' And if you do it another time, it'll change again. For some reason the dream world can't hold on to words in print."

That sounded creepy. What if Carrie opened up her diary, the part she'd written as Mona, and it was all different? But this was about dreams. "What if there's no writing?" Carrie asked.

"You look for other mistakes—or dream signs, they're called. The dream sign tells you that you're dreaming."

"Dream sign," Carrie repeated. Was that like a road sign? CAUTION, SLIPPERY WHEN ASLEEP.

"If each of you tells a dream, I'll try to find a dream sign in it," Mona said.

"Oh, please." Regina sounded weary.

"I'll do it," said June. "I'll tell a dream."

June described a dream in which she was flying a small plane through clouds. She and her copilot—an older woman, a stranger—were looking at a map of the world. "Where are we?" June asked the woman. But the woman just said something like, "The map's not big enough to show you."

That was how Carrie felt. Not on the map, not American, not foreign, not home on the earth.

"Do you know how to fly a plane?" Mona asked.

"Of course not!"

"Did you think it was strange, that you were flying a plane?" June shook her head. "See, that was your dream sign. You were doing something you don't know how to do. Also, you have to be on the map, somewhere. You can't be . . . nowhere. That's another dream sign, when things just don't make sense."

Then my life is a dream sign, Carrie thought, because my life doesn't make sense. Who would have thought her mother could die so young? Was her mother on any map, anywhere? No, she was nowhere. Her mother had insisted on cremation, ashes scattered in the Atlantic Ocean, because it connected America to Europe, where she was born. You're nowhere if you're scattered. They'd taken her ashes out to the beach. Carrie tried to remember that day. Who'd been there? Her father and Mutti, of course. It was almost all gone—except for one thing. It had been a chilly October day; she'd worn her wool winter coat and mittens. But her hands had gotten hot. So hot she'd felt like the mittens were suffocating her hands. She kept telling herself, "Take your mittens *off!*" but she couldn't do it. The word "off" had lost its meaning, becoming only a sound, like paper ripping.

But what she actually said was, "Even missing girls are somewhere. Just not where they're supposed to be."

"I love hearing about missing girls," Regina said. "They're so brave, running off, leaving behind what's safe, no matter what the risks."

Carrie felt disloyal, since she agreed with Mrs. Mendoza that it was "a tragedy." Carrie had to try to keep Mrs. Mendoza on the other side of the generation gap.

"Is the map a symbol for something?" June asked.

"I don't go for that symbol stuff," Mona said. "Symbols are too simple. Nothing's that simple." Nothing was simple? Carrie wondered how Mona could be so sure. "You know, this means that, a key is knowledge, horses mean danger, a house can be different parts of your mind, water is sex—"

"I'll go swimming with Craig Forrest anytime," Regina broke in. "But I think he likes Ruby Stevens. I could strangle her."

"I'll tell a dream," Mona said. Regina folded her arms. "My doctor told me I had a horrible disease, that I'd be dead in one week. I went to a drug store to buy vitamins, but all the vitamins were broken and crumbled. When I showed this to the druggist, he said, 'What do you care? You'll be dead in a week.' See? That was my dream sign. How could the druggist know?"

Carrie wasn't too surprised that Mona had weird dreams.

"Did you catch the dream sign? Did it turn into a lucid dream?"

"No, but it really gave me the creepy crawlies." Mona flushed. "I sound like my mother. Anyway, in the dream, I told my mother that a really expensive operation could save me, but she wouldn't pay for it. She cried in a very phony way at the funeral. This was so much like her in real life, that's probably why I missed another dream sign—seeing my own funeral."

Carrie simply couldn't believe that about Mrs. Brockner. Allowing her own daughter to die!

"Your turn," Regina said to Carrie.

"My turn?"

"This whole dream thing was your idea."

This whole dream thing. Carrie looked at her mother's picture—the sort of smile, the almond-shaped eyes, head tilted back slightly, full, curly hair past her shoulders. Mona was wrong. Carrie's mother looked nineteen and nothing like Carrie.

"Carrie," Regina said. "Anybody home?"

"I've had so many fascinating dreams, it's hard to pick one out." Carrie was stalling and she knew it. She couldn't bear to tell the dreams about her mother, but the trouble was, she couldn't remember any others. Lots of mornings she'd wake up, knowing she'd dreamed, feeling the trail the dreams had left behind in her head, a glimpse of something just beyond her reach—maybe a window with billowing curtains, or a running girl; it didn't seem fair, somehow, to have a dream and then lose it somewhere between *asleep* and *awake*.

"You don't have to do it," June said.

"Oh, but I want to, I really do!" Carrie took a deep breath. "Here goes. I dreamed I was in a meadow. I could feel—something soft under my feet. Grass, soft grass. I began to run. I was being chased. No, something was chasing me. A creature. Large and white and—" She glanced at Regina's sweater. "Furry. It lunged into a cave. I couldn't help it—I stumbled. My shoe hit a rock—"

"But you were barefoot!" Regina's voice was sharp.

"Yes, barefoot. One shoe off and one shoe on, like 'My Son John.'" Carrie felt hot. "Then I began falling, down, down, down. I kept getting smaller, as small as a bug—"

"Oh, please!" Regina sounded disgusted. "Carrie, you're telling us *Alice in Wonderland*."

Carrie stiffened. Truly, she hadn't realized it.

"Maybe this wasn't such a good idea," June said.

"No, it was. It is!" Carrie figured she must be weird herself, wanting this so badly. "Let's all come here tomorrow. I'll tell a real dream then." Though she had no idea where to find a real dream by tomorrow. In all of downtown Belle Heights, she'd never seen a same-day dream service.

"What about you?" Mona asked Regina. "You want to tell us a dream?"

"Tomorrow." Regina got up to go. "Fair is fair."

Mona was the last to leave. She and Carrie stood at the door a moment; outside, dark leaves swirled. "Does it make you uncomfortable?" Mona said.

"Does what make me comfortable?"

"Well, I hate my mother—"

Just like Regina, Carrie thought. But how could anyone hate Mrs. Brockner?

"—and your mother's dead."

Hearing it out loud always gave Carrie a chill, an empty chill. She felt the pit, so big it echoed.

"It's like a rich person telling a poor person she hates money," Mona said.

"Do you feel rich?"

"No. Bankrupt."

Carrie looked at Mona's hands, the fingernails bitten down as far as they could go.

"How is it, living with your grandmother? She seems great, but you never know."

Mutti—great? "You never know"—something Mutti herself would say.

"Do you like it?"

"Yes and no," Carrie answered—exactly how Mutti answered questions. This was like Mutti talking to Mutti! And then Carrie realized where to find a dream by tomorrow—a dream for free, right here at home. And she wouldn't even have to go to sleep to get it.

The War

Chapter 5

"Mutti, tell me about the war."

Mutti almost dropped the soup ladle. "What?" she managed to say.

"Tell me about World War Two."

"But you don't listen. I tell you—I try, time and again—you say you need a nap, or some such thing."

"I'll listen now." Carrie wanted to sound miraculously pleasant.

Mutti filled the soup bowls. "What do you want to know?"

"Stories. Before the war, during the war. Just stories."

"Let's sit and eat and talk. I maked lovely pea soup. With crewcuts."

"*Croutons,* Mutti."

The kitchen wallpaper, chosen by some previous owner, showed butterflies circling tiny plants with red stems and three bright green leaves. It couldn't possibly be poison ivy—who would ever design poison-ivy wallpaper?—but no other plant had those three shiny, green leaves. The soup was delicious, and Carrie said so.

"I did want sauerkraut with dinner, but the sauerkraut here

in America is terrible. In Vienna, almost every street had a vendor. They did fork it out of big vats and put it on newspaper, hot and steaming. You ate it with your fingers."

The only vendor Carrie knew was Mister Softee. She tried to imagine the little truck for Mister Sauerkraut.

"Before the war, life was easy. Too easy! In Vienna—you do know that we lived in Vienna?" Carrie nodded. "Your mother was twelve. With that gorgeous flaming hair and those sea-green eyes, she was the most beautiful girl in a city of beautiful girls. Boys from the *gymnasium*—that's what school was called— did visit always. Your mother maked me tell them she was not at home when meanwhile she was upstairs with a book. Can I wait? the boys did ask. I had to get them out of the house. *Die rote Liesl*—the red Liesl."

Carrie's mother's name was pronounced "*lee*-zull." Carrie, with her round brown eyes and wild brown hair, had always been in awe of how pretty her mother was. And she'd been glad that her mother didn't wear a lot of makeup, or have stiff, mile-high hair, or talk too loud, like all the other mothers. "Go on," Carrie said.

Mutti looked at the poison-ivy wallpaper. Carrie saw that talking about Liesl maybe wasn't the easiest thing for Mutti, even if she wanted Carrie to hear it. "We lived on the second and third floors of a house, a very nice apartment in the Leopoldstadt, such an elegant district. We had crystal chandeliers and handmade rugs and a winding staircase made of oak. We were near the Prater, a huge and beautiful park. No cars did go there, just horses, and there was a Ferris wheel—you can see it in a movie, *The Three Men*."

46

"*The Third Man.*" Carrie wasn't sure how she knew this, because it was an old movie. But she could almost remember something about another old movie, too, one that had once made her mother cry. Maybe she'd heard all this before and then forgotten it. What struck Carrie was that her mother and grandmother had lived in a neighborhood much better than Belle Heights.

"Papa was in the furniture business, kind of a middleman between the factories and the stores." Papa—that meant her grandfather, Mutti's husband, who had died when Carrie was a baby. Carrie's other grandparents were still alive, but felt like strangers; they lived in Florida and sent postcards with palm trees and a gift in the spring, on her birthday. "I was a secretary. At home, I had a Hungarian girl to help me. She cleaned and did laundry and babysat Liesl."

"Wait a minute," Carrie broke in. "Mom told me about that babysitter. She left her off at the movies. Mom saw *Dark Victory* four times in one afternoon. She cried so much, her eyes got swollen and she could hardly see." Amazing, how Carrie could remember something so completely, quickly, out of nowhere.

Mutti tightened her lips. "She left Liesl off at the movies?"

"So she could see her boyfriend."

"I did like that girl. I trusted her!"

"Mutti, don't be mad *now.*"

Mutti smoothed the front of her simple beige housedress. "Yes." She looked steadily at Carrie. "You listen good. I can feel how good you listen."

"Thank you." As for Carrie, she noticed Mutti spoke better,

too, not so many mistakes in her English and not so much German backward talk.

"Yes," Mutti repeated, taking Carrie back with her to Vienna. "You had to shop every day, because there was no refrigeration. But the shopping came to you! Every morning, right at the door, were bakers with their fresh pastries and crispy rolls. In America the bread is soft." She made a face. "In Vienna, the bread was so hard, you could knock on it and hear a fine, hollow sound. It kept your teeth strong. A sign of beauty was good teeth, and we all had excellent teeth. So do you, Carrie. My favorite pastry was a *kipfel*—a horn—and that's what it looked like. That and cocoa was breakfast, the first of five meals every day."

Five meals! Carrie was impressed.

"At ten o'clock you had a small snack called *imbiss*—maybe some herring in cream, a little goulash, a frankfurter. Lunch was the big meal. Vegetable soup, salad, chicken, and pastry. At four you had a little cake and coffee. The last meal was light, just bread and sausage."

So, maybe Carrie's appetite *was* normal—normal for Vienna.

"I had time for myself. I played Strauss waltzes on the piano. I had friends—we went for walks, to museums, to concerts. Vienna was a cultured city, a very beautiful city." Then Mutti's voice slowed down, and got deeper, sadder. "Vienna was a very cruel city, too, especially for the Jewish people. See, Carrie, in Vienna the Second World War didn't begin with guns. It began with a celebration." There was a black line down the middle of Mutti's life, Carrie realized. It reminded her of two kids she knew back in Spruce Hills, who divided their room exactly in half with a line of black tape down the middle of the floor. For Mutti, time was split in two—before the war, and then everything that came after, including now.

"When Hitler invaded Austria on March 11, 1938, people stood in the streets cheering! Many Viennese wore special badges. A white circle around a black swastika, with a red border. That meant you were a Nazi even before Hitler came. It was terrible to see that badge on so many of our neighbors and friends. Just weeks before we had been in their houses to see their Christmas trees. Now they wouldn't talk to us. There was supposed to be an election the following Sunday. Suddenly there was no election. The Cafe Splendide turned into Kaffee Berlin. Policemen became our tormentors. All of Liesl's friends in school, except the other Jewish children, shunned her. No more boyfriends, naturally. Suddenly she was ugly to them, ugly and dirty. I always thought Austrians were not of good character, and I was right."

"But you're Austrian!"

"No. I'm American."

Still, you're not a real American, Carrie almost said. Not like Mrs. Brockner.

Mutti said Jews were rounded up immediately and ordered to wash the sidewalks—political slogans for the cancelled election had to be cleaned away. Mutti scrubbed on her knees, while crowds gathered to cheer and laugh and spit. *Come on,* they sneered, *you can do better.* Liesl had to write *Jude* on shops owned by Jews, while her classmates laughed.

Carrie thought about Lolly, Trippy, Regina, June, Mona. Laughing at her. Of course they were all Jewish, too—practically everyone in Belle Heights and Spruce Hills was. How had her mother handled it so well? To go from being the most beautiful girl to being the outcast.

"We'd heard things were bad in Germany but we didn't believe it. Go to jail, just for being a Jew? Ridiculous! But true. I never imagined we'd have to leave Vienna—after all, Papa did fight on the German side in the First World War. But then came *Kristallnacht.*" Mutti gazed beyond Carrie, like Veruschka, but it wasn't a Future Look, it was a Past Look. "All night, there was shouting and screaming and glass shattering." Mutti sat quietly for a moment, as if hearing the echoes. "The Nazis said a Jew did kill a Nazi in Paris. So they destroyed our synagogues—all the synagogues in *Wien.*"

"Where?" Carrie asked.

"*Wien*—Vienna. They broke the windows and set fire to the buildings. They did call it *Kristallnacht*—Crystal Night—because the broken glass shined so beautifully in the firelight, like crystal. This was November tenth, nineteen-thirty-eight. I will always remember this date."

Carrie wondered if all the race riots this past summer had reminded Mutti of *Kristallnacht.* And she knew the answer. How could they not?

"Nobody went to the window that night. We were so afraid they would come and get us, within minutes. The next morning—" suddenly Mutti started to laugh.

Carrie was confused. "Mutti, what's so funny?"

The next morning, Mutti explained, police went door to door, rounding up people to clean up the broken glass from the beautiful new synagogue on their block. Storm Troopers were the shining examples of the Nazi police force—tall, blond, fit. But this job was left to the lower-ranking Brown Shirts, nicknamed for their uniforms.

When Mutti opened the door that morning, she faced two men in brown shirts who, she said, "looked just like the dumb gangsters you see in American movies. 'Do you have children?' one of them did yell. 'No,' I told him. 'We hear you have a girl,' the other one said, and took a step inside. 'Why, yes, I have a daughter,' I said. Liesl was halfway across the room, hiding behind the couch. The first one demanded, 'Where is she? Upstairs? Get her down here, right now!' I told him, 'But she's only an infant!' From behind the couch, Liesl did laugh, and did cover her mouth with her hands. An infant! She was twelve, five feet nine inches, a strapping girl. 'That's not what we heard,' the second one told me. I began wringing my hands. 'My little Liesl!' I said. 'Such a little baby, asleep in her crib—she's so tiny and sickly, you know.' *Sickly!* Liesl did laugh so hard I could hear her. So I had to cough. 'Do you know a doctor?' I said, between my coughs. 'Could you send a doctor for my sickly Liesl?' The Brown Shirts got angry and left. Liesl still laughed. And I laughed, too."

"Yes," Carrie said. "Mom always laughed a lot. She was such a happy person."

"Carrie," Mutti said quietly. "She was terrified."

"But you said it was funny—"

"I said it made us laugh. I didn't say it was funny."

Carrie got confused again. "You were laughing just now, too. Why were you laughing now?"

"I don't know. I suppose I'm still terrified."

But Mutti was the least terrified person Carrie knew. She looked at Mutti's hands. The skin was wrinkled and thin, the veins as blue as rivers. She almost reached over to touch Mutti's hand—but she hadn't done that for so long, she wasn't sure how it would feel.

Chapter 6

"I dreamed I saw a beautiful girl in hiding," Carrie began, still wearing Regina's black caterpillar sweater, as they all sat on Mutti's couches and ate crispy apples that Regina had brought. "Brutal guards came to the door, asking for the girl, but her terrified mother tricked them, telling them her daughter was only a baby. . . ." Carrie didn't say a word about Vienna or Nazis, and nobody guessed it, either.

"Oh, my God!" June said, when Carrie was finished. "What an exciting dream. Carrie, your mind is absolutely fertile."

Carrie had to laugh. It made her sound pregnant.

"It's vivid," Mona agreed. "I guess your dream sign would be, how could you be a witness? I mean, where were you, Carrie, when all this was going on?"

Carrie shrugged. "Watching, I guess. Like it was an old movie."

"So if you see things that you really shouldn't be able to see, that's a dream sign." Mona frowned. "Actually, I missed my own dream sign last night. I dreamed I had a mysterious disease. In a special mirror I could see my skull. It didn't look like there was anything wrong but the doctor told me I was dying."

"You're always dreaming about dying," Carrie said.

"Dying's not so bad in a dream. It only means part of you is dying. Could be a part you don't need."

"Part of you is *dying?*" Regina said. "Should we have a funeral for the part you don't need?"

Mona coughed. "Or, who knows? I don't go for that symbol stuff, anyway. It might mean nothing."

But Carrie could see that Mona knew exactly what it meant.

"I had a dream, too," June said. "In the dream, I woke up. I remember getting up and out of bed. Then I took a shower and washed my hair. I got dressed, too, and ate Froot Loops."

"You shouldn't eat Froot Loops," Regina grumbled.

"What you had," Mona said, "is called a 'false awakening.'"

Carrie thought about that a moment. Waking up and remembering that her mother was dead—why couldn't *that* be a false awakening?

"Well, here's my dream, and it was seriously scary." Regina pushed up her sleeves, which fell right back down again. "I was one of the nurses in the apartment the night Richard Speck came."

"Oh, my God," June said again. "Regina, why didn't you ever tell me this?"

"It was too awful to talk about."

Carrie had to agree. The summer before, a drifter named Richard Speck had killed eight student nurses in Chicago. It was on TV and in the papers every day for weeks. Richard Speck didn't know his victims; they didn't know him. It was all random and senseless.

"I'm hiding under a bed, all tied up, like that one nurse who survived." Regina wrapped her arms tight around herself. "I can't see all of Richard Speck, just his arm with that tattoo—BORN TO RAISE HELL. Each time he returns, for one girl after another, I see that tattoo. Sometimes I see his eyes—soft and gentle, just like the newspapers said."

"I remember." June shuddered—and so did Carrie.

"Isn't that the scariest dream you ever heard?" Regina was challenging Mona, who didn't respond. "Well?"

"I can't answer that," Mona replied.

Again, Mona was the last to leave. At the door, Carrie asked her why she didn't think Regina's dream was the scariest she'd ever heard.

"Because she didn't really have that dream, that's why."

Carrie just stared at her. "How do you know?"

"Because dreams are . . . funny. If you dream about Richard Speck, he could show up as a tiny piece of dust in your eye. A speck—get it? And writing has to change. Regina said she saw that tattoo over and over."

"It doesn't *have* to change, does it?" Carrie got worried. Did Mona know that Carrie's dream wasn't real, either?

Apparently not—because all she said was, "It can't help it. So one time Regina might have seen BORN TO RAISE HELL, but the next time she'd have to see something else, something like—"

"BORN BLONDE?"

"Oh, Carrie, BORN BLONDE on Richard Speck!" Mona smiled. She had a great smile, like a beautiful old house opening its front door for you.

But maybe Carrie's "dream" was setting off something inside Mona, because she started talking about Mutti again—asking,

When is your grandmother home? Could I talk to her sometime?

Carrie wasn't sure she wanted Mona and Mutti together in
the same room. She remembered that Mona also lived with her
grandmother. "I'd love to talk to your grandmother, too."

Mona hesitated. She was about to say something, Carrie could
see it. But she didn't. Instead, she looked into the overcast sky
and said she had to get going.

Chapter 7

That night, Carrie cleared away the dishes and filled the goulash pot with hot water and a squirt of Joy. Usually Mutti had to remind Carrie about chores—and usually more than once. "Want to soak your feet?" Carrie asked.

"I was off my feet most of today. Orders and bills."

Mutti ran Luncheonette, while the owners lived in Florida; sometimes she cooked or worked the cash register. Carrie had been there half a dozen times, seeing Mutti in a big white apron. Many of the customers seemed to know Mutti well enough to call her Hilde and to know that Carrie was her granddaughter.

In the living room, Carrie pressed her to go on with the story. "We'll talk until the news," Mutti said.

Nothing got in the way of the news.

"In 1939, things did get worse, and continued to get much, much worse. There was still no war, not officially, but there was talk of concentration camps. No one died at these places, not yet. Papa could walk the streets safely because he didn't look Jewish. But one day he got arrested. He came back after six days—beaten, starved, and then let go. Beaten so badly that a scar from a stomach operation years before opened up. Carrie, after this, he was never the same—not right in the head. I had to make all the decisions. I had to do everything."

Word spread about something called *Kindertransport*—the Children's Transport, where you could safely send your children off to other countries. Papa couldn't bear to send Liesl away, but Mutti knew it was absolutely the right thing to do— "I didn't hesitate for a moment." She got on line the day the office opened and got Liesl properly registered, giving the authorities fifty pounds in English money and Liesl's picture.

"*That* picture, in fact. A copy, of course."

"What one?"

"The one on the bookshelf."

Carrie couldn't believe it. Mona was right. Carrie's mother, in 1939, was Carrie's age.

"We waited. Children did go on the fourth of every month. On July fourth, nineteen-thirty-nine, it was Liesl's turn." How American, Carrie thought—the Fourth of July. "Liesl wore a green hat—dark green on the inside, light green on the outside, to set off her red hair. Somebody did give Liesl a brown tweed suit to wear. Everybody at the train station was staring at her, she looked so beautiful. Two girls, ten-year-old twins, were crying—they didn't want to go. Their mother asked Liesl to keep an eye on them. Liesl was such a good soul—she had the girls laughing even before getting on the train."

Carrie thought about how her mother, even as an outcast, was always so strong, confident, cheerful. More traits Carrie had not inherited, along with height, beauty, and elegance.

"Papa made a scene. As the train left, he started to yell, *We're terrible parents! We sent her away! We shouldn't have let her go!* We didn't hear from Liesl for eight days. Papa didn't sleep. I mean, not at all. Finally we got a telegram. Liesl was safe. Then Papa slept."

"Where was she?"

Mutti blinked. "You know, Carrie. On a farm in Scotland—with Angus Fraser."

"Oh, right." For Liesl, a haven. For Carrie, the pendulum. Why did she feel this way? What was wrong with her?

"Angus and his wife, Flo, were so wonderful to Liesl. During the six years Papa and I were separated from her, I did write to her whenever I could, though naturally I never could hear back. After Liesl left Angus's farm, Angus always made sure Liesl got my letters. It was how we found each other, after the war. And I stayed in touch with Angus all these many years. How could I not?"

"Right, right." Carrie nodded, as if she knew all this already. "So what happened next in Vienna?" The part about the train and the twins wasn't bad, but she didn't really have a good "dream" yet.

"One of our Nazi neighbors tipped us off that Papa would be arrested again. Typical Viennese—playing to both sides! We had to leave, but I did want my parents to be safe. I got a job as a nurse—"

"Mutti, since when were you ever a nurse?"

"I did learn. Quickly. Hitler said he didn't want to kill the elderly, that their next stop was the graveyard anyway. I did get a job in an old age home so I could put my parents there. Hitler was lying, naturally. My parents and everyone else in the home were killed the following year in a death camp."

Carrie looked at the lines in Mutti's face, the lines that spoke of the war that had happened to her, really happened, not just in the papers or on the evening news.

"I did give a lawyer money to send us to Bolivia. He took our money and ran away with it himself. Now all we could do was try to escape. On New Year's Eve, with the war on, Papa and I got a ride to the Yugoslav border, and walked across on foot, while the guards were drinking. There were parties everywhere. I wore three sets of closes, one on top of the other. I had maybe ten dollars in my pocket, and of course we had no papers or passports. Any policeman could have thrown us in jail, or worse, at any moment. We walked and walked through snowy villages, past farmhouses. It was early morning, nineteen-forty. No one was outside, but inside people celebrated. I could hear the sounds of laughter and music."

They spent several months in a farmhouse in the Croatian town of Sisak. Mutti saw the movie *Snow White* there—dubbed in Croatian, so she didn't understand much. After that, they had to run from town to town. The Germans occupied Yugoslavia a year later. One day, Mutti and Papa got on a bus, finding seats in the very back. Only moments into the ride, the bus stopped— there was a checkpoint. Guards with rifles got on and walked down the aisle, demanding papers from each and every passenger, and of course Mutti and Papa had none. They sat there and watched the guards get closer and closer—until the guards stood directly in front of them, questioning an Italian woman in the second-to-last row. "This woman was, how do you say it? Feisty. She got into such a tremendous fight with the guards— so help me, I can't remember over what—that they got disgusted and left." The only two passengers on the bus who had not been checked were Mutti and Papa. "It was so terrifying, I can't tell you. To this day, busses still make me a little nervous."

Carrie found it hard to imagine that busses could be anything but incredibly boring.

A month later Mutti and Papa got arrested, anyway, by somebody else in some other place. They were crammed into trucks along with 150 other people and sent to a farm where, Mutti said, they were fed out of buckets, nobody could wash, and there was no toilet. "It was our first of nine concentration camps."

"But you said it was a farm."

"A concentration camp was anywhere you were taken and held. It could be a farm, a school, even a nice hotel—though not so nice when we did stay there!"

When the trucks came again, Mutti said, "We went next to a farm that looked more like a concentration camp, with barbed wire all around."

The first day in the new place, Mutti and her group were given sacks to fill—they had to empty an enormous grain silo. Then they covered the floor with straw and hay; this was where they would sleep.

"Then came the real surprise. Our first night in the silo, we did hear chirping, like birds. But it wasn't birds. We couldn't use candles because of the straw, so we turned on the electric lights, even though the guards might notice. And we saw *them*. Rats. The size of cats. No, bigger than cats. Everywhere."

Carrie thought she might get sick.

"Running along the rafters, over our heads. Running over us, as we lay on the floor. I never heard such shrieks in my life."

"Mutti"—it was hard even to say it—"how can rats get so big?"

"They had all that grain to eat."

Carrie swallowed hard.

"Nobody slept that first night, I can tell you. Some people got big sticks and tried to chase the rats away. In the morning we didn't see rats. Where were they? Sleeping in the rafters. Guards did set up traps with poison but the traps didn't work. Only mice did get caught. By the second night, we were so exhausted, we slept, rats and all. I worried about rat bites but, to tell the truth, when the rats ran over me I didn't care."

Rats ran over that man, too, the one in the Edgar Allan Poe story. Carrie wondered how long it would take her not to care about enormous rats using her like she was Belle Boulevard.

"People put nails into sticks, cut the head off the nail, and filed the end to a sharp point. They stabbed the rats, but you can't kill a rat that way. This is how to do it." As if giving Carrie a recipe for pea soup! "First you put the spear all the way through the rat while it sleeps, into the wood rafter below. If the rat isn't completely pinned down, it runs off. You need two people. One person pins the rat with the spear, the other uses a stick to beat it to death. All this time the rat is screaming, really screaming."

Carrie had to take a long, deep breath. Mutti walking in a beautiful park with horses and a Ferris wheel—she could see this. Mutti as a nurse—she could even see this, too. But Mutti as a member of a giant-screaming-rat killing team—never.

"One day a guard did try to help. He brought in a tiny, pudgy dog. A trained rat killer, the guard said. Well, we laughed. We thought the rats would eat that dog for lunch. But right away the dog ran for a rat, bit its neck right through, and threw the rat over his shoulder. That dog killed dozens of rats every day. But never enough. I found newborn rats in my shoes when I tried to put my foot in. I found baby rats in my coat pocket. We lived with the rats for three weeks. What could we do? We could nothing do."

Mutti stopped. It was time for the news. There were more, many more dead soldiers in Vietnam; a peace demonstration filled Washington; cleanup efforts were underway in big cities. Carrie let it all wash over her like dishwater.

They talked some more, during the commercials, and Mutti took Carrie through another two years of the war. Carrie found she couldn't follow everything, though she did hear that at one point Mutti weighed only eighty pounds. "Hunger hurts," Mutti said. Carrie asked some questions over and over, trying to turn Mutti's stories into stories she could somehow get inside. But real stories told out loud weren't like fairy tales you could snuggle into at bedtime. They weren't like dreams, either, although Carrie had all she needed for tomorrow.

"Enough, enough for now." Carrie felt a little like an overflowing sink. "Oh, I'm sorry, I mean, I'm only listening to it, and you had to live it. How did you live with it, Mutti? How do you live with it now?"

"I don't live with it. It lives with me."

Carrie's mother sat at Mutti's kitchen table, looking down. *Why won't she look at me?* Carrie wondered. *Why won't she talk?* There was something else Carrie was wondering, too. Something she couldn't get hold of, something just out of reach, something she was supposed to say or do. *This isn't what I think it is,* passed through Carrie's mind. But she didn't know what else it could be, if it wasn't simply what it was.

Waking up Carrie realized, with a start, that she'd come as close as a breath to lucid dreaming.

Chapter 8

Yesterday's clouds had blown over and it was cold and brilliantly sunny, but dark enough in the living room for a bear to happily hibernate. Mutti had rearranged the couches; she did that sometimes. Now they formed a *V.*

"I had a dream," June said, "and it had Regina in it."

Regina let out a smothered laugh. "Not a seriously scary dream, I hope?"

"I gave you something," June told her. "My sandwich. Tuna fish, I think. You said you wanted one small bite. So, okay. But you kept on eating and eating it. You ate the whole thing."

"But I'm the one who always gives *you* food!" Regina said.

"This was in my dream," June said carefully. "I got upset. You just said something like 'I kept forgetting it was yours, and then there was only one little bite left, so I went ahead and ate it, because I forgot again and thought that was the bite you wanted me to have in the first place.'"

Regina fidgeted in her seat.

"It wasn't my first dream about you," June said. "Another time I found you in the bathroom at school. You were crying, really crying, like a little kid. I asked you what was wrong.

You said you had a secret, a terrible secret. You told me, 'I'm in eighth grade—but I'm really only nine years old.'"

That was how old Carrie had been when her mother died.

"Another time I dreamed that Dinah, your cat, ran away. We looked and looked all over for her. We found her, finally, in a pet store. But she had a different name—'Buddy,' I think it was. Or maybe 'Skippy.' You didn't want her anymore. You said she was too different now—"

"I can't stand it!" Regina said. "Don't you have any dreams without me?"

June seemed to shrink into herself. Carrie felt a little bad. The four of them had had such a good time at lunch, eating Regina's nectarines and coming up with dumb ideas for "The Earth Is Our Home" projects. No question about it, the dreams were causing problems.

"Well," June said, "the woman in the plane wasn't you, and then there was my 'false awakening' . . . and another time I dreamed I was at school, doing something in science lab. I was alone. No, wait, there was this guy in a lab coat. He said he could show me life on other planets. He said—what did he say?—to meet him somewhere. In front of the A&P. At midnight. I was so curious that I went. It was seriously scary at first. A lot of weird guys hang around the A&P at midnight. And then, suddenly, I don't know how, but everything changed. I stood in sunshine, on a dirt road. I walked along the road and then there was a little village with huts. And people in long white robes. They offered me something. Bread—good bread, I had it in a restaurant once, real bread, not that stuff you usually buy at the A&P."

"I hope you accepted," Mona said.

"Why's that?"

"Because anyone you meet in a dream could be a dream friend. Dream friends can rescue you if you're under attack, or help you find your way home if you're lost. And accepting a dream gift from a dream friend is the best thing that could ever happen in a lucid dream."

Carrie almost cried out, "That's it!" She could make a dream friend and get a dream gift. It was her first real goal in so long.

"Well, I took the bread." June grinned. "The guy from the lab asked me, did I like this place? I said it was great, but where are we? He told me we were in the exact same spot, right near the A&P. I didn't understand. He said something like, 'Life on other planets is right here on earth, but in other dimensions.'"

"June, you have the best dreams!" Carrie said.

"No, I like yours!" June said.

Regina shot her a look.

"What do you think it means?" Carrie found herself asking Mona.

Mona shrugged. "Maybe that something can look as boring as a bus stop or an A&P, but when you look at it another way, it turns out to be something else, something totally unexpected."

Carrie nodded. "And wonderful."

"And wonderful," Mona agreed.

"We're not supposed to interpret dreams, *remember?*" Regina said.

"I remember," Carrie said, and was just about to tell her "dream" about the rats, when Regina broke in, "A missing girl was murdered, you know." Regina sat on the edge of the couch. "It just happened. I read about it and saw it on TV. The girl—

her name is Linda Rae Fitzpatrick—ran away from her family's mansion in Connecticut and was found dead in the East Village."

June looked confused. "Hold on. Is this a dream?"

"Of course not! This isn't some silly dream. This is life, real life. Linda's house had ten fireplaces and nine bathrooms. She went horseback riding. Her mother bought her a new wardrobe every season."

"Sounds more like a life you'd run away *to*," June said. Carrie could see she was trying to get into the spirit of it.

"Her teachers in Connecticut said she was just a nice, normal, happy little girl. One of her hippie friends in the East Village said that Linda thought she was a witch and could fly away on a broom."

Why is she telling us this? Carrie wondered.

Suddenly Regina was staring at Carrie, eyes blazing. "Why not?" she demanded.

"Why not what?"

"Why don't you want to hear this?"

Carrie hadn't realized she'd said anything out loud. "It's just so sad. A girl runs away—a missing girl—and instead of finding someplace that's safe, I mean, some people have to go away, so they can be safe, but all that happened to this girl was that she got killed."

"You'd rather talk about dreams?" Regina asked, though it didn't sound like much of a question. "Dreams are *nothing*, they're not real—"

Carrie couldn't breathe for a moment. It was as if Regina was saying that Mutti's entire life wasn't real. "But my dream *was* real," Carrie said carefully.

There was silence. Carrie glanced at Mona. Mona had no expression at all. Then June said, "That thing with the guards, and the girl who was hiding? Oh, my God!"

"Don't be silly," Regina said. "You were never chased by any guards."

"It wasn't me. It happened during the war, to my mother and grandmother."

"The grandmother who lives here?" June said. "Oh, my God!"

"So." Regina spoke in a low voice. "You lied."

"Well—" It hurt, admitting it.

"We were nice to you, Carrie," Regina said. Carrie noticed that instantly she wasn't part of that "we" anymore. "You didn't have any friends here in Belle Heights. I loaned you my best cardigan—which, incidentally, I'll take back, thank you very much."

Carrie slipped it off and handed it over. She wondered if she'd ever feel anything that soft again.

"You betrayed us," Regina seethed.

"Hold on," June broke in quietly. "I wouldn't put it that way—"

"She betrayed us." Regina got up to leave. "Let's get *out of here.*"

June looked at Carrie. Carrie could see it in her eyes. Long before Carrie had come to Belle Heights, Regina and June were friends, and Regina was letting June wear her sweaters, and

Regina was making sure June didn't eat the wrong things. Carrie told June, "Don't sweat it."

Which was funny, since Carrie was sweating all over. What was wrong with her? Normal people had normal goals—to change the world, or make the swim team. But getting a dream gift from a dream friend—what kind of goal was that? How could she just let June and Regina walk out—leaving her with weird Mona, who was watching all this as if watching TV?

"I'm not sure what just happened," Carrie said, as the door clicked shut behind them.

"I bet it happens all the time. I know her type." Then Mona said something about a bus stop.

"A bus stop! You mean, where we met? What's that got to do with anything?"

"A bust-up," Mona said carefully.

"Oh." A tongue-twister. Bus stop, bust-up. She had a bus stop with June and Regina.

"It wasn't much of a beginning," Mona said, "and it wasn't much of an ending."

Carrie eyed her carefully. "You don't sound too surprised. I mean about my dream."

"I guess I'm not." Mona shrugged. "I'm not sure why."

"Or too betrayed, either."

"No," Mona said. "So tell me about your grandmother. Who were the guards? Who was the beautiful girl?"

After Carrie had told her, Mona said, "What a life your grandmother's had! But I've got to go now. There's stuff I have to do at home—"

"So, could you teach me?" Carrie asked urgently. "How to lucid dream. I want to learn."

"I can try. It's like anything else, Carrie, like math. You have to do homework."

"I'll do homework. I'll do anything."

"Why are you so interested?"

Carrie didn't know. "But you must be, too, or you wouldn't know so much."

Mona breathed out. "It's the kind of thing that's the best part of . . . now. Opening up your mind. Trying to figure things out. Looking around at what's out there, and what's in here." Mona tapped her forehead.

Now Carrie's goal didn't sound so silly. As for Regina and June, she would miss June, and she would miss Regina's sweater, but she would definitely not miss Regina. Carrie walked Mona to the door.

"I need to go now—"

"It feels like a pit," Carrie said, as if the fact that there was no time to say it made it okay to say it. "My mother being dead. It's all hollow and empty inside—" she wrapped her arms around herself, "and all the sounds echo without fading away." Carrie remembered that her mother did this, too. Talked when there was no time to talk—running late, rushing off. "People visit you, but they're only next to the pit. No one's inside the pit with you. Then they go home and you're still in the pit." Carrie stopped short. Why was she telling this to Mona?

"Are you saying you feel like there's a pit inside you, or that you're inside the pit?"

Carrie hadn't thought about it too clearly. "Both, I guess, if that makes any sense."

Mona nodded. "So, what you're saying is, you'd like someone inside the pit with you."

Carrie didn't know if she was saying that or not.

"I could go in the pit."

Carrie just stared at Mona. Had she heard her right?

"Even when I'm not here, I could be here. Does that make any sense?"

Carrie nodded. Maybe these things made their own kind of sense—the same way you could feel like a missing girl without running away.

Am I Dreaming?

Chapter 9

Skin cells, Carrie wrote in her looseleaf, *are irregular and loosely packed, like kids in a schoolyard. Onion cells, on the other hand, are tightly packed, like the subway at rush hour. In an onion cell, the cell wall is on the outside and the cell membrane is on the inside of the outside.*

The inside of the outside. That was exactly how she felt, more like a new kid now than on the first day of school. She changed her homeroom seat, way over to the back wall, between posters of the South Pole and the North Pole (part of "The Earth Is Our Home" exhibit). Glancing toward her old part of the room, she saw June, head down and scribbling away, and Ruby Stevens, feeling Regina's fluffy sweater. It reminded Carrie of cotton candy—something that looks real but, when you touch it, melts into nothing.

Carrie had lunch with Mona.

She told Mona about how Mutti had killed giant screaming rats during the war. "It would have made a great dream," Carrie said, almost wistfully.

"It's better as real life, though for your grandmother's sake I wish it had been just a dream." As they stacked up their trays on a tall pile that threatened to topple, Mona asked, "Want to come to my house this afternoon?"

"Will your mother be home?"

"No, thank God!"

The chill in the air was gone and the afternoon was warm and mild and clear. Carrie liked it when the seasons didn't get so stuck inside themselves, when you got a day like this, summer in the fall. She even liked wintry days in the spring.

Mona's slate-roofed, two-story house had red brick and creamy plaster walls and a rectangle of bright green lawn out front. It looked exactly like an old English cottage, except that it was next to, but not attached to, another English cottage, and another, and another, to the end of the block. Carrie had never seen these houses before, like something out of a fairy tale; it was strange, because Mutti lived on the same street, just farther down.

Once inside, Carrie was struck by how much light filled the rooms, as if they faced the sun on all four sides. She could hear birds, something that never happened at Mutti's. Everything smelled like a garden, fresh and flowery. There was thick carpeting everywhere—not exactly red, not exactly orange. A sunrise color. In the living room, there was a plump, soft-looking crushed velvet couch beneath a large mirror, and the coconut-brown wallpaper looked three-dimensional. Carrie touched the wall; it felt scratchy. "What's this?"

"Grasscloth."

"You mean—grass from the lawn?"

"It's a different kind of grass."

There were tall bookshelves crammed with hundreds of big,

shiny art books—paintings by Picasso, Matisse, Chagall. Carrie flipped through a couple and recognized some of the more famous paintings, but when she opened the Van Gogh book, there was a spectacular one she'd never seen before. "Blossoming Almond Tree," it was called, thin gnarled branches with delicate white flowers against a blue sky. The thick, blue brush strokes looked almost like a basket weave, all folded over onto themselves. The book said Van Gogh had painted the sky first. Carrie would have liked to have seen the painting when it was like that—all sky, only sky.

There was a maplewood entertainment center with a big color TV, an expensive-looking stereo with big speakers, and cabinets for stacks and stacks of records. Everything looked new, brand-new. There were paintings on the walls, too, elegant reddish shapes and swirls. "Where'd you buy the art?" Carrie asked.

"My father paints."

"You mean . . . your father's an artist?"

Mona shrugged. "It's just a hobby."

But Carrie was impressed.

They went into a gleaming kitchen with an enormous two-door refrigerator. There was a white Trimline phone on one wall—the cord was so long it almost touched the floor—and, high up on hooks, were enough pots and pans for three luncheonettes. Spices Carrie had never heard of filled a blond wood rack—cardamom, turmeric, coriander, marjoram. Carrie and Mona sat on white stools behind a shiny white counter; up on a shelf, Carrie noticed a mug that said WORLD'S BEST MOM. "Want some Coke with ice?" Mona asked.

Carrie couldn't believe it—there was an ice-making machine inside the refrigerator! When Mona gave her the tall, slightly gray-green glass, Carrie noticed the ice smelled a little funny—but still . . . "I bet your freezer is self-defrosting, too. Mutti's freezer turns into one big ice cube. I have to stab it with a knife."

"Like it was a giant rat?"

"Yeah, and it screams the whole time." A pile of mail lay on the counter. "I see you have a prescription to *Life*."

"Prescription?"

Carrie flushed. Here she was, born and raised in America—sounding like an immigrant! "*Sub*scription, I meant."

"I know."

Runaway Kids was the cover story, photographs of girls and boys with their eyes covered by black rectangles. *"We love you, call collect, Mother and Dad,"* was the caption beneath one picture.

"Regina must be in heaven," Carrie said. "All those missing girls to read about."

"Regina doesn't care about missing girls."

"Sure, she does! She said she admires their bravery—"

"She only cares about being the center of attention. Believe me." Sometimes Mona sounded so much older than thirteen. "You know, Regina really hated it when June liked your dreams. Because June didn't rave about Regina's dreams."

"But Regina only mentioned the one dream—"

"Doesn't matter."

What Mona was saying sounded right, but Carrie had to ask, "Mona, how do you know that?"

Mona shrugged. She just knew.

Carrie flipped through the magazine, glancing at the letters to the editor. Under the heading "Veruschka" was a little note: *"Life" in the article mistakenly added more than four inches to Veruschka's height.* So, Veruschka wasn't six feet, four inches? She was less than six feet? Not an entire foot taller than Carrie, after all.

". . . it self-defrosts," Mona was saying, when Carrie tuned in again. Now she was doing with Mona what she usually did with Mutti.

"Who does?"

"Not who—what. The freezer. Self-defrosts."

Right. She'd asked about that earlier. "So that's good. You don't have to defrost it, then."

"I have plenty more to keep me busy." With that, Mona removed a note on the refrigerator that had been carefully folded under a Snoopy magnet.

Carrie read it, clearly written in perfect, straight, up-and-down letters:

> *MONA*
>
> *THURSDAY*
>
> *Defrost ground veal*
> *Change sheets—Grandma's room, too!*
> *Sinks are yucky*
> *Run the dishwasher*
> *Math test tomorrow*
> *Love, Mom*

"It's . . . kind of a lot." But Mrs. Brockner must be a very busy working woman, or she wouldn't be giving Mona all this to do. And, on second glance, things like defrosting ground veal and running a dishwasher took only a moment, anyway.

"Every day there's a new list. Sometimes it's really nothing, just picking up something from the dry cleaner's. Sometimes it's like this. That's why I always have to be home by five."

"I bet your mother has a good reason why she doesn't hire a cleaning lady."

"It's a stupid—but convenient—reason. She doesn't want strangers in her house, touching her things. Also, it's a daughter's duty, right? My mother, a psychologist, a career woman! But a dinosaur at home." Mona shook her head. "I can't believe when I was little I used to beg, please let me help you with the dishes! I just liked being near her. She smelled so good. She still smells good. But, believe me, I don't want to be anywhere near her now—"

"I'll help you," Carrie said quickly.

"You don't have to. Really, you don't. I can get it all done when you leave."

"It's okay," Carrie said, and she meant it. Funny, to still feel a little awkward with Mona, but to want to spend time in her house, learn it by heart.

As they scrubbed the kitchen sink, Carrie saw why Mona's hands always looked so red and raw. This, and the nail-biting. She really should wear rubber gloves.

Over the clunk and roar of the dishwasher, Mona explained "waking signs."

"It's the homework part, Carrie. Imagine any three things that could happen to you in a day. Looking in a mirror. Smelling cigarette smoke. Mrs. Mendoza calling on you. Any time one of those things happens, ask yourself, 'Am I dreaming?' And tell yourself, 'No, I'm not dreaming. I'm awake.'" Mona paused. "So, pick three waking signs."

"Okay. Three waking signs. How about—seeing streetlights turned on at night?"

"That's good."

"And putting a key in a lock."

"Very symbolic—if you're a symbol person. A key is supposed to be knowledge, remember?"

But Carrie liked it as a waking sign, symbol or not. Anyway, she felt as if these waking signs were picking her instead of the other way around. "Seeing a woman in a green hat."

"What made you think of that?"

Carrie shrugged. "Did you buy your mother that?" she couldn't help asking, pointing up at the mug that said WORLD'S BEST MOM.

"Are you kidding?" Mona laughed, the way people laugh when they don't think something is funny. "My mother bought it for *her* mother."

If Mrs. Brockner thought her own mother was the world's best mom, then that woman must be extra-extraordinary.

Upstairs, the bathroom had a tiled shower stall in that same sunny color—which Carrie now thought of as "Brockner Red." And a fuzzy cover on the toilet lid (she hadn't known such a thing existed). And a round scale with large, easy-to-read numbers. Carrie got on. Still 126 (she subtracted two pounds for clothes and shoes). Mutti had a scale, too, but it was broken. Carrie weighted 60 pounds on it.

Everything was so clean. All of the Brockner Red towels had "B" monogrammed on them. What exquisite taste Mrs. Brockner had! Behind the mirror, Carrie saw a bottle of Born Blonde. She tried not to feel disappointed that Mrs. Brockner dyed her hair, that she took the time to do that instead of maybe helping Mona around the house.

At the end of the hall, behind a closed door, Carrie heard the smothered sound of a television.

"That's Grandma Rosie's room," Mona said.

"Too bad she wasn't a flapper, with a name like Rosie." It fit, that this lovely home had somebody named Rosie—World's Best Mom.

"I'll go in there by myself," Mona said. "It's better if my grandmother meets you when my parents are here. You can wait in my room."

But which room was Mona's? Carrie was faced with two doors, both closed. She opened the closer door, and saw a bed that was definitely not Mona's, a queen-size bed with a curved wooden headboard and a Brockner Red bedspread. No chairs, but two night tables. A couple of paperbacks, nothing like the books downstairs. These looked like historical novels, girls on the cover in Pilgrim outfits. There was something sexy about the girls, something Carrie didn't normally associate with Pilgrims.

Carrie couldn't help noticing her reflection in the huge standing mirror. She changed the angle so the mirror looked down on her; she looked thinner that way. But this exposed a pile of stuff behind the mirror, things that needed putting back in closets or bureaus. In Regina's room, piles were everywhere, all out in the open. Here, the mess was hidden.

On top of a large bureau there was a row of fluted perfume bottles. Carrie smelled each one. Lilacs, roses. They smelled, if anything, too strong; the scent was more subtle on Mrs. Brockner herself. There was nail polish, too. Cherries in the Snow, Pink Dawn, Sunset. Carrie tried not to think about how she was a stranger, touching Mrs. Brockner's things. Did my mother wear perfume? Carrie wondered. She couldn't even remember that.

Suddenly she felt the pit open up inside her and had to sit on the bed (which was super firm). Then, on the bureau, she saw a key, a tiny key, like the one for a diary, or maybe a mailbox. Carrie thought about Mrs. Brockner picking up the tiny key and opening a shiny metal lock to get her mail. A key in a lock, one of Carrie's waking signs.

Am I dreaming? No, I'm not dreaming, I'm awake.

And Carrie remembered—no, her mother never wore perfume. It actually made her sneeze. She was very sensitive to smells. Her skin was super sensitive, too. She had to buy special unscented soap. It cost extra.

"Here you are!" Mona called out, arms full of sheets for the Brockners' bed.

They changed the sheets in Mona's room, too. Clearly Mrs. Brockner had done all the decorating, except for a touch of Mona here and there. Mona had the same Brockner Red carpeting, and twin beds along one wall, head to head, with matching patchwork quilts. Two beds—all ready for sleepovers. Carrie hoped Mona would invite her to stay over sometime. Sleep here, in the Brockner home, and wake up, still in the Brockner home.

On top of Mona's bureau was a small turntable with a stack of Beatles albums.

"Just the Beatles?" Carrie said.

"There is no other music. I can't listen to anything else." Sometimes Mona sounded so black-and-white about things.

An overhead light was covered with a Japanese lantern that gave the room a soft, fuzzy glow. From the window, you could see several tall trees and somebody's back terrace. On Mona's wall, instead of posters of cute kittens or spirals to make you dizzy, there was a photograph of the profile of a horse.

"Did you cut that out of a magazine?" Carrie asked.

"It was in *Life*. My father took it."

"He's a photographer, too?"

"Like the paintings. Just a hobby."

"My father doesn't have hobbies. He barely has time for his life."

Chapter 10

It all got arranged instantly. Mrs. Brockner came home, wearing a chic red-and-white paisley linen dress and a wide-brimmed hat, heard from Mona how Carrie had helped all afternoon, and invited—no, insisted—that Carrie stay for dinner. "All that hard work deserves a reward!" Mrs. Brockner said, with her pleasant smile. "Mona, it'll be such fun! It's the first friend you've had over since forever."

When Carrie called Mutti from the kitchen to ask—no, to say—that she was eating dinner here, Mutti said, "Are you all right, Carrie? I did so want to be with you on this hard day."

Carrie had no idea what she was talking about. Hard day? Probably some Vietnam thing, or another riot in a city far away from Belle Heights. Carrie also didn't want to think about how disappointed Mutti had been the night before. *No stories tonight,* Carrie had told her. *Enough—enough for now.* "It's a lovely day." Carrie twirled the luxuriously long Trimline cord. "I was practically sweating on the way over."

As Carrie hung up, Mrs. Brockner told her not to play with the cord. "It gets all tangled," she explained. "Then we can't walk as far as we might need to."

"I'm so sorry!"

Mrs. Brockner wore pale, dusty powder on her face and smelled of lilacs. She placed both hands so firmly on Carrie's shoulders that Carrie wondered if fingerprints would show up later, through her sweatshirt and everything. "Don't be silly, dear. Mona used to do it all the time. Now she doesn't."

In the spacious dining room (Mutti had a small dining room that she hardly ever used), they sat at an oval table set with delicate flowered plates, a white linen tablecloth, and real cloth napkins. So elegant! So unlike what Carrie was used to! She felt like a misplaced left shoe that had finally found not only its right mate, but even the beautiful box they'd both arrived in.

Mr. Brockner, who sat at the head of the table, was, no question about it, the best-looking older man Carrie had ever seen. Gentle blue eyes, a round face, full lips, and hair as straight and brown as Mona's. He'd come home in a suit but was now in a striped T-shirt and khaki pants.

"Upstairs I saw your picture of the horse," Carrie told him.

"Oh, that!" He laughed. But even when he wasn't laughing, his eyes crinkled at the sides. "Would you like me to take your picture after dinner?"

"Oh, Tom, that sounds like fun!" Mrs. Brockner accepted for her.

Usually Carrie didn't like to have her picture taken—in all her class pictures, she wore a bright white blouse and had a strained smile. But Mr. Brockner was so nice. *Tom.* What a lovely American name. "It sounds great," Carrie said. "What kind of work do you do? I know Mrs. Brockner is a psychiatrist—"

"Psychologist," Mrs. Brockner corrected her.

"Right." Carrie didn't really know the difference, but was mad at herself, anyway.

Mr. Brockner said, "I'm the art director at an ad agency."

Carrie observed his long, pale fingers. These hands took pictures, painted paintings. An artist's hands.

Mona's grandmother sat across from Carrie and Mona, quietly eating her stuffed green pepper. Wearing a flowery Japanese-style robe, and a huge, tight, shiny metal belt like some medieval torture device, she looked a lot like Mrs. Brockner, only of course much older, with blue eyes that were too close together and gray hair that looked windblown (though as far as Carrie knew, she'd been in her room all day). While Mrs. Brockner talked about how they'd seen *Bonnie and Clyde* at the movies ("That ending! Really gave us the creepy crawlies"), and also *Hair* at the Public Theater ("The nudity was tasteful, thank heaven"), Carrie got the feeling that Mona's grandmother wasn't listening to the words, only their rhythms.

"And I've been reading about that Shoeneck girl," Mrs. Brockner said. Carrie looked at her blankly. "Elizabeth Shoeneck." Mrs. Brockner spoke with emphasis, as if this girl were as famous as Elizabeth Taylor. "She's a missing girl. Well, officially she's a routine runaway girl, but her father's a bigwig in the Republican party and I can assure you there's nothing routine about the entire police force combing the East Village for her."

It didn't bother Carrie, hearing Mrs. Brockner talk about

missing girls. In fact Carrie admired how well-rounded she was, not so war-obsessed like Mutti.

"She left a note for her father, but he wouldn't reveal what was in it. Mona, if you ran away, what would your note say?"

"I wouldn't run away," Mona said simply.

"But if you did," Mrs. Brockner pressed her.

"If I did, I wouldn't leave a note."

"Oh, you're no fun! Carol, how about you? What would you write to your mother?"

Carrie looked at Mrs. Brockner, positive this was one of those "right times." She said, "My mother died."

"Oh, you poor thing!" Mrs. Brockner's eyes softened. "For a child to lose a mother at such a young age, especially a daughter . . . when, dear?"

"Four years ago—today." It hit Carrie, like a meteor. So that was what Mutti had meant. Carrie should call her right away, and apologize—

Mona said, "Carrie, I didn't know it was today."

"I almost forgot it myself. It wasn't a day like this one. I mean, today's like the Fourth of July." But not the same Fourth of July, of course, as the day her mother left Vienna. "That day, the day my mother had to leave home—I mean, the day she died, was cold and dark." But Carrie didn't want to go into details, not during this lovely dinner. Also she could see that Mona's grandmother was listening to her, really listening. "Mmm, this meal is—the best!"

"Why, thank you, Carol!" Mrs. Brockner sounded as if no one had ever complimented her cooking before. "Some ground veal, onion, bread crumbs—poof, finished, couldn't be simpler."

Poof, finished. Carrie's mother used to say that, too. It always made things sound so effortless. "Would you like another stuffed pepper?"

"Thank you, yes." Talk about stuffed! "And the salad—it has radishes—"

"Carol, you're easy to please."

That was news to Carrie. It would have been news to Mutti.

"By the way, Tom," Mrs. Brockner said, using an enormous fork to hold up Carrie's stuffed pepper, "have you seen my mail box key?"

"I have!" Carrie said, happy to help. "It's right on your bureau, next to your Cherries in the Snow nail polish."

Mrs. Brockner stopped what she was doing, stuffed pepper in midair. Her shoulders tensed. And the look in her eyes. As if Carrie were a thief. "You were in my room?" she said, too quietly.

"Mother, we were both in there together," Mona broke in. "Changing the sheets, remember?"

"Changing the sheets is one thing." Mrs. Brockner didn't say what the other thing was.

"Carrie wasn't trying on your underwear and reading your dirty books!" Mona snapped.

Carrie felt herself cringe.

Mrs. Brockner took a deep breath, relaxed her shoulders, and scraped the stuffed pepper onto Carrie's plate. "It's fine," she said, after a moment. "Thank you, Carol. Now I know where to find my key."

Everyone sat in silence for several moments as Carrie ate. She badly wanted it to be fun again. She asked the Brockners, "How did you two meet?"

To Carrie's relief, Mrs. Brockner laughed. "Carol, how sweet that you want to know. It's all so boring and silly, of course. We both went to Brooklyn College and met at a frat party. How boring and silly can you get?"

Carrie loved it—she could have eaten it up like a third stuffed pepper. So American!

"We married when I was in graduate school—"

"So you weren't a psychiatrist yet."

Mrs. Brockner straightened her back. "No, dear, *psychologist*. I've told you—more than once, I believe."

But it was only once, wasn't it? Still, why couldn't she get this right, already?

"Let me explain. Psychiatrists are medical doctors. They go to school for many years more than I did."

"You don't need more school. You're the smartest person I ever met."

"Oh, you're sweet."

"No, I mean it. Mona's been telling me about lucid dreaming and how it all came from you." Carrie glanced at Mona. Had she said too much? But Mona didn't seem to mind.

"Ah, lucid dreaming," Mrs. Brockner said, as if it had been a favorite vacation spot. "I never could do it myself. During the seminar, we were supposed to keep a dream journal. Mine was always blank. I could never remember my dreams."

"Me, neither!" Carrie said.

"I tried, Carol. Before I went to sleep, I told myself, *You will remember*. I'd go to sleep counting, one, I am dreaming, two, I am dreaming, three, I am dreaming—"

Carrie laughed.

"It is funny, isn't it? Instead of counting sheep, counting off and telling yourself to dream! The professor told us that in the morning, when we woke up, we shouldn't move a muscle. He said that trying to remember a dream in the wrong position is like writing with the wrong hand."

Mr. Brockner was smiling at his wife.

"I'll try it," Carrie said.

"Feel free," Mrs. Brockner said. "Though I must warn you, it never worked for me."

"That's because all of your dreams have come true," Mona's grandmother said.

Carrie stared at her. It was kind of an odd thing to say. But, she supposed, it could be nice, too.

"Oh, Grandma Rosie." Mrs. Brockner waved her away. "Carol, what I'm learning now is even more exciting." Her eyes brightened. "How to hypnotize people and cure all their problems. In one case, a young girl who'd been lonely her whole life was hypnotized and, while she was under, her therapist invented a friend that came to visit her every Saturday. He was called 'the Saturday man.' When she woke up after each session, she felt a little less lonely."

"Like a dream friend," Carrie said.

"No, it's different," Mona broke in. "This hypnosis thing sounds dangerous. What if some nut says something weird to you when you're unconscious? How can you defend yourself?"

"The therapist has to be very, very careful." Mrs. Brockner

stood up. "Now if Carol's going to be photographed, we'll have to get her ready."

"Please, let me help clear the table first." Carrie was already gathering the plates.

Carrie rinsed while Mona loaded up the dishwasher. Carrie had never seen the inside of one before—it looked like some bizarre, colorless coral reef. "You have such a nice father," Carrie said.

Mona shrugged. "He's all right."

"Oh, no, he's much more than all right!"

"Well, he married *her*. Hand me that strainer, will you?"

"You mean the colander?"

"I didn't know you knew that word."

Carrie felt stung. "I'm not an immigrant. Just because I said 'prescription,' and didn't know what grasscloth was—"

"Carrie, I didn't mean anything by it." Mona looked surprised. "Besides, what's wrong with being an immigrant?"

Everything, Carrie thought. "Nothing," she said.

As Mona folded the tablecloth, and Carrie scrubbed the kitchen sink for the second time that day, Mona's grandmother came up noiselessly behind her. "They'll be drafting teenage girls soon, you know," she whispered. "You'll be going to 'Nam. Could get a leg blown off."

"Excuse me?" Carrie felt warm breath on her neck. As she turned around, Grandma Rosie was walking away.

That's crazy, Carrie thought. She's crazy! But maybe she'd said the kitchen was drafty, and Carrie had heard it wrong. Anyway, so what if Grandma Rosie said weird things occasion-ally? Lots of old people did that. Not Mutti, not even occasion-

ally, but lots of other old people. After all, this was a perfect family. Well, not perfect, of course, but close enough.

"Come!" Mrs. Brockner called to Carrie from the plush
couch. She was holding a hairbrush and a Brockner Red
cardigan.

"She doesn't have to wear that," Mona said.

"It's okay," Carrie said. "I like it." First Regina loaned her a
sweater, and now Mrs. Brockner. For a moment it felt as if
Regina were really Mrs. Brockner's daughter, or maybe a younger
version of Mrs. Brockner. Which was ridiculous, of course.
They didn't even know each other.

Carrie put the cardigan on over her sweatshirt. Right away
she felt scratchy and hot and lumpy, but she kept it on. It
smelled like lilacs. She sat down and sank into the couch, which
was so soft she thought it might swallow her up.

"That color gives your face a glow," Mrs. Brockner said.
"Your black sweatshirt with your olive skin, oh, spare me." She
brushed Carrie's hair back—way back. Why did she have to do
it so hard? The brush had bristles like a porcupine's quills, and
Carrie's eyes watered. "This is such fun! Mona won't let me
touch her. She thinks I have cooties."

Mr. Brockner used a camera that was so big it covered his
whole face. Carrie didn't know what to do—put a dandelion between her lips?

"Smile," Mrs. Brockner said. "Show off that dimple!"

Carrie sort of smiled at Mona, who didn't smile back. She
heard a loud *click*.

"Won't that make a lovely picture, Grandma Rosie?" It
sounded odd, Mrs. Brockner calling her own mother "Grandma."

But then, Carrie called her own grandmother "Mommy" in German.

Grandma Rosie was frowning. "The furniture's all wrong. What happened to the furniture?"

Carrie was the only thing different about the furniture.

"Oh, Grandma Rosie! It's where it always is!" Mrs. Brockner was about to pull the sweater off Carrie when she hesitated. "Oh, why don't you just keep it."

Keep, not borrow. Carrie was so touched.

"And now it's time to say goodnight, Carol."

"But I'm not tired!"

"It's a school night, dear. Mona has a math test tomorrow—no doubt you have homework, too. I hope we'll see you again."

"Of course we'll see her again!" Mona broke in. "What do you think?"

"Carol, are you as whiny to your mother as Mona is to me?—oh, I'm sorry, I forgot." She reached over and hugged Carrie, rock hard. Carrie felt Mrs. Brockner's ribs beneath the smooth linen of her dress.

"Thank you," Carrie said. "For the sweater, for the dinner, for everything—Rochelle."

Mrs. Brockner pulled back. There was a harsh look in her eyes. Why was Carrie always messing up? "Do you call your own mother by her first name, Carol?—oh, dear, I did it again."

"It's okay," Carrie said. "It's easy to forget. Like the way I keep thinking you're a psychiatrist. Besides, I'm the one who's sorry—Mrs. Brockner."

Mrs. Brockner finally smiled again. "It's fine, dear. No apology necessary."

Mona said she would see Carrie tomorrow. Then she headed upstairs, not saying goodnight or anything to her parents. If Carrie were Mrs. Brockner's daughter, she'd make sure to get one of those hugs every night, even if it did take her breath away.

Mr. Brockner walked Carrie home. Outside, streetlights were on. *Am I dreaming?* Carrie asked herself. *No, I'm awake.* Mrs. Brockner was right—Carrie did have homework. Her waking signs.

"We love this neighborhood," Mr. Brockner said, as they turned the corner. "It's so peaceful in such a troubled world. You can forget all the rest of it."

"I love it, too." Carrie didn't mention how it felt like nothing instead of something, or how Mutti, right here in Belle Heights, never forgot.

"I'm glad Mona has a friend like you," Mr. Brockner said.

Carrie felt his hand on her shoulder. What if people passing by thought this man was her father? They'd be mistaken, of course, but what a great mistake. "I'm glad, too. Your family is perfect." She could feel herself blush. "Well, not perfect, I mean—you know what I mean."

Mr. Brockner laughed. "I'll be sure to tell Mrs. Brockner. She's proud of her family."

At Mutti's door, Carrie put her key in the lock. *Am I dreaming? No, I'm awake.* What a crazy choice, Carrie thought, remembering her third waking sign—a woman in a green hat. She'd probably never see one.

Mutti, on the couch, was in tears.

"Mutti!" Carrie felt awful.

"It's not what you think. I'm watching *The Days of Wine and Roses* on TV."

Mutti had said it right, but for some reason Carrie heard it wrong, as if she'd said, "I'm watching *The Day of Whine and Rosie.*" Mutti had moved the couches again; now they were opposite each other. *The furniture's all wrong,* Grandma Rosie had said.

"Did you have a good time? What did you eat? Did someone walk you home?"

It was heaven! The food was lovely! An artist walked me home! "I had a good time. We ate stuffed peppers. Mona's father walked me to the door."

"Carrie, don't answer like I'm homework. Talk to me." She squinted. "Is your hair different?"

"Not so different." Carrie would wear her hair like this all the time. Once upstairs, she wondered, should I go back downstairs and have a real conversation? Instead she got into pajamas and wrote in her diary. *Hi, it's Mona. Carrie came over. My mother brushed Carrie's hair. My father took Carrie's picture.*

There was a knock at her door. She slipped the diary under the covers. "Come in."

"Your father's on the phone. It's a bad day, for him, too, and he thought you might like to talk—"

"Thanks, Mutti, but I'm half asleep." Carrie knew her father preferred his dark cloud of silence, anyway. She closed her eyes and rolled over, wrapped tight in her blanket.

Chapter 11

Carrie dreamed.

She and her mother sat at an oval table with an elegant linen tablecloth. Everything was in black and white; Carrie's mother wore a gray tight-waisted wool dress with a high collar, the kind of thing that would be way too hot for Carrie and wouldn't fit her, anyway. Carrie's mother looked down at her lap.

"Are you safe?" Carrie had no idea why she'd asked that.

Liesl rested her hand on the table. Her fingernails were actually in color—a shiny pale peach.

Of course! Carrie remembered it perfectly, as if someone had shown her a snapshot. Liesl always wore peach nail polish. "I have to tell Mona," Carrie said. "I'll tell her as soon as I wake up."

That was when Carrie realized she was awake inside her dream.

Am I dreaming? Yes, I'm dreaming. She felt a surge inside her, like a giant wave—it almost knocked her down. *It's happening—it's really happening.* She was having a lucid dream, something even Mrs. Brockner never had. Don't wake up! she ordered herself, somehow knowing she was on the verge of losing it. *Don't wake up.*

"I have a new friend. Her mother is so nice, you'd like her so much. But I'm not supposed to twirl the phone cord or call her by her first name. But she braided my hair"—that didn't sound right, but Carrie couldn't think how to correct it—"and her father painted me." That wasn't right, either. Something else was wrong, too. What was it?

Of course. She'd failed to realize it all those years in all those dreams, but now that she was awake while asleep it was as clear as a window. Carrie's mother was dead.

So who was this person sitting across from her?

"It's not really you, is it? That's why you won't talk, why you won't look at me. You're telling me, without really telling me, that you're not really here, that I don't really have a mother."

Liesl finally looked up at Carrie, smiling gently, sorry to disappoint her.

It rained all day, straight rain like lines. Mrs. Mendoza talked about Venus, how its atmosphere was so dense it bent light in weird ways. You could, for instance, see the back of your own head, the image of it having completely circled the planet.

At lunch, over meatloaf and a mountain of mashed potatoes, Carrie told Mona all about her lucid dream.

"Let's write it down," Mona said. "You're supposed to write down your dreams and give them titles. That way you'll never forget them." Carrie wasn't so sure she wanted to remember this one. "We'll call it 'Nail Polish,' how's that?"

Fine, Carrie thought. That was better than "Carrie's Mother Who Turned Out Not to Be Carrie's Mother." She noticed that Mona was writing down the dream in her own looseleaf. But that seemed fair. After all, Carrie wrote Mona's diary entries in her own diary.

"The dream made you feel bad, didn't it?"

Carrie nodded. "But waking up wasn't so hard. So that part was better."

"Lucid dreams are supposed to make you happy. Maybe it's because, in a lucid dream, your conscious mind and your unconscious mind are one. It's like the two halves of your head are shaking hands."

Your head shaking hands? Maybe on Venus! Carrie looked down at herself. She was wearing a black pullover and black jeans, as if going to a very casual funeral. She'd forgotten all about the Brockner Red cardigan—the dream had pushed it away. From now on she vowed to wear it every day.

"But it was a thrill, wasn't it? Lucid dreaming?"

Carrie agreed that it was—a big thrill.

"You know, there's something interesting you can try next time you dream about your mother."

"She's not my mother."

"Whoever she is, next time you see her in a dream, you can ask her questions. Things like, who am I? Who are you? What do I need to know? And next time try to get a gift."

Carrie could have kicked herself. Even in her dream, she was messing up. The bell rang; they got up to go to class. And something came to Carrie with the same surge of excitement she'd felt in the dream, only this time she didn't have to worry about waking up. "Mona, she's not my mother—she's a dream friend."

At the cafeteria door, they stopped. "My mother had skin cancer," Carrie said. "I thought that meant the cancer was all over her skin. Her skin was so sensitive—she even used special soap. It's stupid, but I used to wish the cancer had been someplace else, like her liver, where I couldn't see it." Carrie was doing it again, talking when there was no time to talk. "The summer before she died, there was a lump, like a hard-boiled egg, on her thigh, near her hip. It was taken out. From August to October she mostly stayed in bed. She had a flowery quilt—I loved that quilt. No, wait, maybe I didn't. When I crawled under it, I got too hot." Carrie could feel herself frown. "My mother got thinner and thinner. I thought she would disappear. But she didn't. Except in my head."

Mona took hold of Carrie's hand. Mona's hand felt cool. All around, kids rushed to where they were supposed to be.

"The thinner she got, the fatter I got. Some nights I ate two entire dinners. Not because it tasted good. In fact I couldn't taste anything. More skin, I needed more skin, so I wouldn't get skin cancer, too. Some logic, huh? Now I know all about skin cells. Insides, outsides. She went to a hospital at the end. She talked a lot, those last days. Since there was no time to say anything, that made it okay to say it. But what did she say? I can't remember. She had an accent, but not like my grandmother's. A little softer somehow, like it came from some other place. I should've taken notes, or taped her—my father has a tape recorder. When somebody dies, you don't get much in the way of leftovers. Last time I saw her, her eyes were closed. I thought maybe she was dead. I said, 'Mom?' and her eyes opened. Then she died, with her eyes open. You can tell right away when someone is dead. They leave their body behind like it was a paper bag their lunch came in." Carrie looked at the cafeteria, nearly empty. No paper bags, just trays. "My father was there. He couldn't talk to me or even look at me. He still can't. When I got home that day, I didn't cry. I even felt happy—so happy! I don't know why. It caught up with me a little later, of course. I got sad, sadder than sad. But I never told anyone about that first feeling, not a soul, not my two best friends, not my grandmother."

"Your grandmother would understand."

"How could she? This was her own daughter."

"She had to kill giant rats, right? She'd understand."

Mona sounded so sure, but Carrie had never looked at Mutti that way. "My mother's been dead so long already, it's hard to believe she'll still be dead years from now. Can't people just be dead for a while?" Despite Mona's cool touch, Carrie's hand got a little sweaty. But she didn't pull away. "Without really thinking about it, I keep thinking I might see her at the bus stop or run into her on Belle Boulevard. Without looking, I keep looking for her. I wonder if she'll call me."

"She'd love to call you. She just can't get to a phone right now."

They had to go to the office for late passes.

Heart of Hearts

Chapter 12

It didn't take long for Mona's house to feel like home. Now that she'd helped clean almost every inch of the place, Carrie could have passed a test on it—including questions on Grandma Rosie's room, which they straightened up one afternoon when she was out. With its flowery wallpaper and curtains, single bed, tall bureau, and large color TV, it seemed more like a hotel room than a Brockner bedroom.

Dinners were always a treat. Mrs. Brockner cooked fancy recipes from magazines—stuffed cabbage, croquettes and crepes, baked stuffed haddock—that looked just like the pictures. Carrie always had seconds. She stuffed in the conversations, too—though it was best not to talk to Grandma Rosie, even if she was harmless. When Mr. Brockner told Grandma Rosie she looked nice in green, that "it suits you," she said, "Suits? I should wear green suits?" And she didn't want ice from the ice machine—she said it turned water into something "bad." But between meals, the blurred hum of the television from behind her closed door was the only sign that the house even had a fourth person living there. It was easy to forget about Grandma Rosie.

The only disappointment was the fact that, despite counting

herself to sleep every night, and not moving an inch every morning, Carrie couldn't remember a single dream.

"I just read about a wonderful new idea for a game show," Mrs. Brockner said one night in late October. "It's like *The Newly-wed Game,* only it's called *The Newly Pregnant.* They ask three pregnant women questions about how to raise children. Then their husbands have to match the answers. The winners get full layettes and things for the baby. Honey—" she smiled at Mr. Brockner, "I wish we'd been on that show. We'd have made a killing."

"What do you know about raising children?" Mona said.

Carrie gave her a look. What kind of remark was that?

"What I meant," said Mrs. Brockner deliberately, "was that your father and I agree with each other so well, we'd have matched all our answers." She paused. "No need to act out, Mona."

"Anyway, the show sounds like a big flop."

"I'll watch it," Carrie said.

"Of course you will—we all will! And maybe you girls will be on it someday."

"I'm never getting married," Mona said. "Never having children."

Carrie knew how black or white Mona could be. Mona meant this.

"I'm looking forward to at least three grandchildren, so don't disappoint me!" Before Mona could reply, Mrs. Brockner went on. "There's still no news about Elizabeth Shoeneck. I wonder where she is?"

That night, after Mona went upstairs and Carrie was getting

her hug from Mrs. Brockner, Mrs. Brockner said, "Would you like to sleep over soon, Carol? Mona asked me about this some time ago, but it's so much nicer now that we all know you better."

"I'd love to—it would be the highlight of my life!" Carrie got embarrassed that she'd said this out loud.

"You're sweet, Carol. You know, I had a best friend once. We were closer than the average bears! Absolutely inseparable."

"Where is she now?"

"Gosh, I don't know. She moved away. I haven't seen her in decades. That's what happens to best friends, Carol."

"Not always. I'll know Mona forever." Carrie was a little surprised at herself. It was the kind of thing Mona might say.

Mrs. Brockner said lightly, "Time will tell." But it sounded as if she already knew what would happen and didn't need time to tell her anything.

Chapter 13

"What's this, moving day again?" Mutti asked as Carrie stuffed her things into a duffel bag.

"I'll only be at Mona's for a night."

"So many closes. Why three pairs of pants, and two night-gowns, and who knows how many sweaters? And look at all those socks!"

It was true. Carrie wanted to take everything. Turn this room back into the storage room it longed to be.

"Does Mrs. Brockner mind that you're sleeping there?"

"Of course not! It was her idea!" Actually, it was Mona's idea, and it had taken Mrs. Brockner a little while to agree to it, but never mind.

"She's always feeding you—"

"Mutti, I don't eat up all her food!"

Mutti wore a housedress with huge yellow butterflies, much bigger and more yellow than any butterflies found in nature. She looked worried.

"It's okay." Carrie tried to sound miraculously pleasant. "I help out at the Brockners'. Do the dishes and stuff."

Mutti still looked a little worried.

✻   ✻   ✻

When Carrie got to the Brockners', Mona led her upstairs. "I've emptied out a whole drawer for you." It was pulled out and waiting.

Carrie piled her clothes into the bureau. Mona's things smelled like baby powder. What a nice smell, like a happy childhood. Carrie even felt bold enough to put her toothbrush alongside everybody else's in the bathroom. Carrie's was plain and green. The Brockner toothbrushes, all different colors, were extra long with rubber tips.

Downstairs, Mrs. Brockner had left them a Saturday list. Instead of "MONA" at the top, it said, "GIRLS." It made Carrie happy just to see that. Some mail was piled up on the counter. Carrie even pretended that a couple of envelopes at the bottom were addressed to her.

There was only one chore: go to Kips, the finest department store in Belle Heights, and get monogrammed face towels—in Brockner Red, of course. Mutti didn't own face towels. One big towel covered everything.

On the swervy bus ride downtown, Carrie looked out at the unending rows of small, ground-floor stores, the huge redbrick apartment buildings with tiny square windows towering above the stores, and the small patches of smoky gray sky you had to crane your neck to see. Everything was still so new; Mutti had told her that most of Belle Heights had been built after the war. Mutti herself was older than her own neighborhood.

A tall girl got on the bus. Her denim jacket was covered with all kinds of buttons. Peace buttons, anti-Vietnam buttons, and one or two about LSD.

"I want to cover myself with buttons, too," Carrie said. "I could wear one that says, 'Am I Dreaming? Yes, I'm Dreaming!' And how about, 'Missing Girl—Try to Find Me!' What would you put on, Mona?"

Mona said she didn't go for that button stuff.

They got off at Main Street and walked for a couple of blocks, passing Army-Navy stores with cardboard boxes full of clothes out front, fruit stands, a fancy shoe store called Shoes to Boot, and Darla's, an ice cream parlor with a famous concoction called "The Kitchen Sink"—thirty-six scoops of ice cream plus all the toppings.

At Kips, it took Mona only a moment to find the Brockner Red face towels. It felt odd to see an entire Brockner Red section, with curtains and tablecloths and soap dishes.

Outside, Carrie and Mona passed Max-A-Million's, the other big department store in Belle Heights, run-down and sad, the opposite of Kips. They stopped to stare in the windows. Most of the mannequins had no arms at all, and the clothes were truly awful, lots of ruffles and huge belts and screamingly loud colors. "Venus de Milo Fashions," Carrie said, and Mona smiled. Then Carrie got an idea. "Let's go inside. We'll split up for ten minutes, and see who can put together the most hideous outfit. The winner gets to choose anything she wants from Darla's, including the Kitchen Sink."

"You mean—for fun?"

"Of course for fun! What do you think?"

"It doesn't really sound like fun."

"You'll see. It'll be great. Only don't look too obvious, and don't laugh, or we'll get thrown out. The salesladies in that place are worse than Mrs. Mendoza."

"Carrie, I don't think I'm going to laugh."

"Don't be so sure."

"Anyway, we can't eat an entire Kitchen Sink."

"Speak for yourself."

They separated in Ladies' Sportswear. Right away Carrie struck gold—baggy multicolored striped pants and a billowing polka-dotted top. She saw an enormous belt made of lizard scales, but it looked too much like something Grandma Rosie might actually wear, so she didn't use it. In the dressing room, Carrie put on the clothes and admired her reflection. Hideous, all right. Perfect!

But when she left the dressing room, there was Mona—who had chosen her outfit even faster. Carrie stood as still as a mannequin in the middle of an aisle, staring, unable to move. Irritated customers brushed past her. Mona had on a low-cut, tiger-print tank top, green velvet culottes, a pink sash, and a beige safari cap. She was glowing and gorgeous, all curves and bare shoulders. She'd thrown back her hair; Carrie, with her hair back, too, the way Mrs. Brockner liked it, knew that it only gave her a big forehead. Had Mona somehow put on makeup?

"Hideous, right?" Mona whispered.

What was hideous was that Mona was already a woman, and Carrie still looked like a little girl, a girl who'd sneaked into her mother's closet. Though of course Liesl's taste had been far more subdued, and there was no closet anymore. All of Liesl's clothes had been given away to the Salvation Army. Carrie got mad about it now. She could have saved some things—for Mona. A saleslady with stiff yellow hair shot Carrie a disapproving look; then she saw Mona and nodded.

"Should I purchase these garments or not?" Mona spoke in a high, fluttery voice that didn't sound like her at all. "I don't have all day." Carrie had to bite her lip. Don't laugh, she ordered herself. "Do you think Craig will like me in this?" Craig Forrest, the boy Regina had a crush on. Carrie burst out laughing. "You're impossible!" Mona said, still in that voice. "How can I buy anything when I'm with you!"

"May I help?" the saleslady asked.

"No, thank you, but you're very kind," Mona told her graciously.

Carrie felt herself wither beneath the saleslady's glare. She followed Mona back into the dressing room. Even Mona's walk was different! No question about it, Mona could easily be a real actress.

After they'd changed back into their regular clothes, they walked down the clunky wooden steps of the broken escalator. "You won," Carrie said.

"I'm not so sure. Those big pants—"

"Don't remind me. Well, I hope you're hungry."

"Not for the Kitchen Sink. Maybe just for the faucet."

At Darla's, they had to wait, but the place was so cheerfully noisy they didn't mind. They ended up at a booth beneath a colorful poster of a circus performer, and read the menu.

"I'll have a piece of lemon meringue pie," Mona said.

"It's my treat," Carrie reminded her. "Get something better

than that." Meringue, like cotton candy, was one of those foods Carrie couldn't get excited about.

"It's exactly what I want."

Carrie got the banana split. At Darla's, it was extra special, with four scoops of ice cream and tons of chocolate topping and nuts and whipped cream.

"Mona, you're an actress."

Mona looked confused.

"Back at Max's. You were amazing. For one thing, you looked beautiful—"

"Oh, spare me," Mona said—and then made a face. "I sound like my mother."

"You changed into somebody else back there. Your voice, your walk, even your face. Isn't it great, to already know exactly what you want to do in life?"

"Who says I want to be an actress?"

"Here's something I once heard—if someone can say, convincingly, 'I love you,' then she can act. Now pretend you're saying it to Craig Forrest."

"Carrie, I don't even like Craig Forrest."

"Try," Carrie pressed her.

Mona looked directly at Carrie. In a steady, strong, thoughtful voice, she said, "I love you, Craig." Was there the hint of a tear in her eye?

"Wow, you're an actress, all right. And I can be your manager." Where had that come from?

"Carrie, that doesn't sound like much fun for you."

But for Carrie, being the manager of the glamorous and talented Mona Brockner felt exactly right.

* * *

They took a different route back to the bus stop. Tucked away behind the department stores was a cluster of houses built more than one hundred years ago—the only truly old places in Belle Heights. These big, bedraggled homes were still beautiful but they'd been cut up into apartments, and rents were cheap.

"I love these houses," Mona said, as they passed a three-story house with peeling green paint and clothes hanging out on a clothesline. "Maybe we can live here someday. Share the rent."

"We'll be able to afford a lot better than this. We can move to Hollywood."

"I'd like to live right here. Everything we need is within a couple of blocks. We wouldn't have to take the bus anymore."

"That's true."

"And we'd save money by getting all our clothes at Max's—"

"Oh, spare me!"

"—and we could listen to the Beatles every day, and eat ice cream for breakfast, and let dishes sit in the sink!"

Carrie looked at the green house. She imagined herself living here with Mona, maybe taking off three or four decades in the middle of her life to get married and have a kid or something, but then growing old with Mona, her best friend.

Chapter 14

Back home, Mona went into the kitchen to rinse dishes for the dishwasher. This wasn't on Mrs. Brockner's list; it didn't have to be. Carrie told Mona to put on rubber gloves. "If you're going to be an actress, your hands can't look so red, and maybe you should stop biting your nails—"

"Carrie," Mona cut her off, "why don't you go upstairs to my room? I'll be there in a minute."

On the stairs, Carrie ran into Grandma Rosie. Whenever she saw Grandma Rosie, she tried telling herself this was a good thing, that she was happy to see her.

"Your mother called," Grandma Rosie told Carrie.

Carrie got a sudden, deep ache. *She'd love to call you, she just can't get to a phone right now.* A moment later—infinitely long inside; a split second on any clock—she realized that of course Grandma Rosie had meant Mutti.

"Thanks for telling me." *You're supposed to be in your room,* she couldn't help thinking.

"I took down your number." Grandma Rosie had put on red, red lipstick; it covered too much of the skin around her mouth.

"But the number is too short. Maybe we should look it up. Do you know your last name?"

"Everything's fine," Carrie said.

"It's not right, having a phone number that's so short."

Just then Mrs. Brockner came home. Carrie spun around, rushed to the door, and gave her a hug. Usually Mrs. Brockner was the one who hugged Carrie, at the end of the visit, but Carrie couldn't help herself. Mrs. Brockner, she noticed, always felt so strong. Carrie wondered if she took vitamins or something.

Mrs. Brockner pulled away and adjusted her clothing. "Such exuberance!" she said, as if it were a cold you didn't want to catch. She took a step back and extended her right foot. "Do you like my new pumps from Shoes to Boot?"

"Oh, yes."

"And my new coat—very warm, nylon filled with polyester, only twenty-five dollars."

"Where'd you get it?" Carrie admired the shiny red jacket.

"Kips. My favorite. I stopped in after tennis."

"We were there, too! We might have run into you!" But if Mrs. Brockner was going there herself, why had she asked them to buy the towels? "Mona," Carrie called out. "It's your mom, and she bought something at Kips, too!"

Mona, in yellow dishwashing gloves, came out.

"You're dripping." Mrs. Brockner pointed at the yellow gloves. "Mona, why didn't you do the dishes earlier? There was a bowl with tuna in the sink. You know bowls with tuna mustn't sit in the sink! They'll smell like tuna forever!"

The phone rang. Mrs. Brockner sighed as she followed Mona

into the kitchen. Then she stuck her head out. "It's for you," she told Carrie.

"Your mother," Grandma Rosie said from halfway up the stairs. Why hadn't she moved? "Good thing she called back."

Carrie got the phone from Mrs. Brockner and took it around the corner into the dining room. "What," she whispered.

"I did call you before."

"We just got home. Mutti, what do you want?"

"You never did tell me Mona's grandmother is crazy! She asked about my accent. I told her I did come from Vienna. She said, 'Hitler's not dead. They never found his body. He wants the Jews in America.'"

"Mutti," Carrie whispered even more softly, "she's Jewish, too."

"That's what she told me! She said Hitler follows her and goes where she goes. Carrie, that woman isn't right in the head. She belongs in a hospital. Why does she live there? Didn't you tell me Mona's mother is a psychiatrist? Doesn't she know better?"

"Psychologist," Carrie corrected her. "There's a difference."

"Anyone with a head on her shoulders could see this woman needs a hospital! What's wrong with those people?"

"Nothing!" Carrie cupped her hand over the phone. "They're working on it. She's going on really strong medication." Carrie had to lie. What if Mutti said she couldn't visit the Brockners anymore? Especially not now, when she was about to sleep over. Sleep, and lucid dream, and remember it word-for-word in the morning . . . oh, no! She'd been twirling the phone cord. She

117

hadn't realized. She unravelled it quickly. "Mutti, why did you call me?"

"It's actually wonderful, Carrie. Angus Fraser did call. He's coming day after tomorrow and will stay for almost a week."

"Day after tomorrow! You said November!"

"The day after tomorrow is November first."

Carrie felt sick. This was even worse than the cord. The pendulum was low, right on top of her now. When she listened in again, Mutti was talking about how Carrie's father had changed his plans around and would be arriving the same day as Angus.

"But I'm not ready," Carrie blurted out.

"Carrie, there's nothing for you to do."

Carrie heard her quite clearly, but in her mind Mutti had said something else. *You can nothing do.*

"They found that Shoeneck girl," Mrs. Brockner said at dinner, placing a stuffed Cornish hen on Carrie's plate. "She wasn't in the East Village, after all. She was in—of all places—Yellow Springs, Ohio!"

"What was she doing all this time?" Carrie was feeling better, reminding herself that this was her home, her real home. Whatever happened in Mutti's house, whoever came and went, had nothing to do with her. Maybe the Brockners would adopt her someday. She was already half an orphan, after all. Carrie Brockner. That sounded nice. Mona had that extra bed, and Carrie's toothbrush was already in the toothbrush holder. . . .

"Elizabeth Shoeneck's family isn't breathing a word," Mrs. Brockner said. "They're keeping her away from reporters, away from everyone."

"It's the worst possible punishment for a missing girl," Mona said. "Keeping her prisoner in the home she tried to escape from."

"You don't know that," Mrs. Brockner said. "Studies show—"

"What studies?"

Mrs. Brockner laughed. "Mona, I don't have a card catalogue in my head! But I do know that children who run away do best when they are returned to their parents. It's familiar and comforting to be back in their own rooms with their own possessions, especially things from childhood."

"You're making this up. You don't know what you're talking about."

Mrs. Brockner sat up straight and spoke quietly. The huge fork she held looked like a pitchfork. "I don't see why you need to act out, Mona."

"I'm not acting out. I'm acting." Mona winked at Carrie.

Keep me out of this, Carrie wanted to say.

"I know where that girl was," Grandma Rosie said. "Right here, in Mona's body. Mona was the real missing girl." She took a huge bite of Cornish hen.

"Mother, it's worse and you know it," Mona said angrily. "As bad as before."

Mrs. Brockner was turning—well, Brockner Red. "You know perfectly well I've had Grandma Rosie evaluated by experts—"

"You call those idiots experts!"

"That's enough." Mrs. Brockner exhaled deeply and closed her eyes. Carrie had the feeling she was trying to hypnotize herself. *Ten, nine, eight . . . calm down.* A vein in her neck stuck out.

Grandma Rosie lowered her fork. She glared at Mrs. Brockner. "What are you trying to do to me? Why did you put aspirin in my food?"

Everyone looked at her.

"Don't think I don't know it, little miss. You thought you could get away with it, but I know you put aspirin in this fat pigeon."

Mrs. Brockner spoke with an effort. "What makes you say that, Mother?"

"Because I'm hot."

"That's it," Mrs. Brockner said, and to Carrie it felt like Belle Heights had just shifted on the terminal moraine.

"Honey," Mr. Brockner said.

"No." Mrs. Brockner's eyes were fixed on Grandma Rosie. "Everything has to be nice. That's what she's always said—my whole life! Nice and clean! Well, I cook! I cook gorgeous dinners! Tom could take a picture of this dinner for a magazine! I've made a nice home. The nicest! I work—I work hard. How can I be expected to work and clean, too?" She waited a moment. Was somebody supposed to answer that question? Her voice got higher and louder. "I took her in. When no one else would have her, would even speak to her, I took her in. Like a good daughter! Like the best daughter!" Then the tears started. Carrie didn't want to hear this or see this. The person who said these things, the person shaking and crying like a child, all sobs and hiccups, wasn't really Mrs. Brockner. It couldn't be. Mrs. Brockner was glacier solid.

"Let's go upstairs." Mr. Brockner enveloped her in his arms.

Carrie wished she could wrap herself around Mrs. Brockner, too.

Mrs. Brockner nodded wearily. Then she looked at Carrie. It was as if she'd completely forgotten Carrie was there, and had trouble even remembering Carrie's name. She narrowed her eyes. "Carol," she whispered, and then, louder, "I want her *out of here.*"

For a moment Carrie thought Mrs. Brockner couldn't possibly be talking about her. It was a mistake, a big mistake, such a big mistake you could laugh about it. Mothers didn't do this kind of thing, right? Her own mother would never, ever. And Mutti wouldn't, either. Or maybe Mrs. Brockner was just saying a weird thing, the way Grandma Rosie did. Like mother, like daughter.

Mona was close to tears herself. "It's not Carrie's fault."

"She's always here! Every time I turn around! It's as if she lives here! How can I be expected to support—I want her *out!*" Like the Red Queen—*off with her head!* The Brockner Red Queen. "Tonight she goes home."

Mr. and Mrs. Brockner went upstairs. Grandma Rosie went back to her meal as if nothing had happened. For several moments Mona and Carrie just sat there and stared at each other. Carrie felt so bad, she couldn't even eat. The pendulum was practically on top of her. She wanted to run away. But not very far. Only to here, to Mona's house. *Tonight she goes home.* It didn't make any sense. This was Carrie's home, too, or at least it was supposed to be. Now she was banished! Like some character in a fairy tale. *Dear Diary,* she would write later. *It's Mona.*

My mother did a bad thing. She—No, Carrie couldn't bear to write it.

"My mother—she's humiliated," Mona said finally. "You saw her lose it. If I could do something, I would—"

"It's okay," Carrie said, though it was absolutely not okay.

"I'll come over tomorrow with your stuff."

Carrie wondered if Liesl had felt this way, leaving her home in Vienna. No, she was all "chin up," getting the ten-year-old twins at the train station to laugh. Liesl was on her way to Angus Fraser, and now Angus Fraser was on his way to Carrie.

Mr. Brockner walked Carrie home. Snow fell lightly, like baby powder. Mr. Brockner didn't say a word. Sometimes he and Carrie walked back to Mutti's house in companionable silence, but this was different. Why wouldn't Mr. Brockner assure Carrie that everyone, deep down, still liked her? Why not crack a little joke to put her at ease? Would it be too much trouble to put a hand on her shoulder? There was something not-quite-there about Mr. Brockner, she realized, as if he were only a photograph.

"I don't see any stars tonight, do you?" Carrie asked, pathetically. Of course you never saw stars when it snowed, not to mention that Belle Heights was too polluted, anyway.

But Mr. Brockner remained silent. Carrie saw only his profile.

"Do you think there'll be another teachers' strike?" No answer. "My grandmother thinks it's getting worse in Vietnam. . . ." Even Carrie stopped listening to her own words.

She put her key in the lock. *Am I dreaming?* She didn't bother to answer. "Mutti?" she called out in the living room. There was a large bowl of candy near the front door. Of course. Tomorrow was Halloween, the night before Angus Fraser's arrival. Somehow that seemed appropriate. "Mutti, where are you?"

Mutti was upstairs, in Carrie's room.

Reading Carrie's diary.

Carrie was horrified. "Mutti, how could you?"

"You're home!" Mutti was so startled, she dropped the diary. "You were staying the night at Mona's! What happened?"

"How could you?" Carrie repeated.

"I was straightening up, and I saw this diary—"

"*My* diary! You should know, you gave it to me!"

"Yes, but I thought maybe you did give it to Mona. I did just pick it up, Carrie. I looked only for a second. Why do you write as Mona?"

"Stop it." Carrie actually put her hands over her ears. It sounded like she was as crazy as Grandma Rosie. "You had no right! This is just like in *1984,* when Big Brother read people's diaries!"

"Well, I'm your grandmother, not your older brother—and I'm sorry, Carrie, I looked only for a moment. But why do you say that you're thirty-two years old?"

It took Carrie a moment. Then she remembered. Veruschka was a 96, Mona a 90 (though she could use a raise, after this afternoon), Carrie a 32. . . . "I was just playing around. Mutti, you had no business reading that!"

"Carrie, why do you want to be Mona?"

I don't, Carrie almost said. I only want to be her manager.

Chapter 15

Carrie stayed in bed all morning. What else was there to do? She didn't want to be asleep or awake, so she drifted somewhere in the middle.

Mona came over that afternoon, Carrie's duffel bag over her shoulder. "It's cold outside but no snow. Have you been in bed all day? You must be hungry."

"I'm not hungry."

"Your grandmother let me in. She invited me over for lunch. She's making some soup—it smells heavenly! How come we were always at my house and hardly ever at yours?"

Carrie didn't answer that. Wasn't it obvious?

"I like your nightgown, Carrie."

"It's old." Carrie's mother had bought her this flannel night-gown covered with farm animals. It had always been big on Carrie. Not any more.

"She told me about Angus Fraser and that he's coming to-morrow."

"I don't want to see Angus Fraser." But suddenly that didn't sound right. "No, wait, that's backward." Like the way Mutti talked sometimes. "This is what I mean. I don't want Angus Fraser to see me."

"Why not?"

"I don't know." Carrie hugged her knees to her chest. *Why didn't she want Angus Fraser to see her?* If it were a test question, she'd have to leave the answer blank.

"I really like your grandmother, Carrie."

"You don't even know her."

"I feel like I do."

"Well, I know your mother very well, and I think she's . . . wonderful."

"You're kidding. She just threw you out of the house, re-member?"

Actually, Carrie had trouble remembering. When she tried to picture Mrs. Brockner's expression from the night before, she could only see the saleslady at Max-A-Million's. "Your mother didn't really mean it." But Carrie remembered Mrs. Brockner's voice. *I want her out of here.* "She won't always be mad at me, will she?"

"She's not exactly self-defrosting."

"She likes me. I know she does." Carrie frowned. "I mean, if she didn't, I wouldn't feel the way I do around her . . . awake in-stead of asleep, is the only way I can put it."

"She's your false awakening, Carrie."

Carrie opened her mouth, but nothing came out.

"She looks real but she's not. When you wake up, you'll know the difference."

"Mona, I'm awake. What are you talking about?"

Mona walked over to the bed. She looked taller, as if she'd actually grown since that first day at the bus stop. "Let's go downstairs and get something to eat. Afterward I'll tell you something about my mother, now that you're ready to hear it."

"Who says I'm ready?"

Downstairs, Carrie noticed that Mutti had cleared off all the bookshelves, except for Liesl's picture, to make room for Angus Fraser's belongings. The couch was now in a straight line—a bed for Angus Fraser. The pit in Carrie's stomach felt like the Grand Canyon, the pendulum so low she could feel the breeze it made.

"I love your kitchen," Mona said. "It's cozy, like an extra friend."

Carrie almost told *Mona* to wake up. "This kitchen is dark and cramped and ancient. It's got poison-ivy wallpaper. You've got a huge new refrigerator with an ice machine and a wall phone—and that light, so much light! It's like the sun is rising right in the middle of your house."

"Exactly. It's blinding."

Mutti gave them steaming bowls of thick goulash soup. Mona took a spoonful and sighed. "This is the most delicious thing I've ever tasted," she said.

Carrie didn't see why Mona had to gush like that. After all, she didn't even like food. "Your mother's a pretty good cook, too."

"Carrie, it's all for show."

Mutti sat and tucked a paper napkin into the collar of her blue and yellow striped housedress. "This goulash soup—" Mutti said "goulash" as if it had three syllables—*goo*-laa-shuh, "did come from my grandmother."

"So that would be . . . Carrie's great-great-grandmother. What's in here? Potatoes, green beans, peas, carrots? Mutti—" it was strange, hearing Mona call Carrie's grandmother *Mommy*. "Carrie's told me about your life. It's so interesting—and so scary."

"This is true. We never did go to a death camp, thank God, but we had our troubles nonetheless. I did tell Carrie the story up to the time my husband and I joined the Yugoslav underground."

"Why did you stop there?" Mona asked.

Mutti looked at Carrie. Carrie didn't feel like explaining. "It just seemed like the right place to stop," Mutti said.

"Why don't you start again? I'd love to hear it."

Carrie figured she simply wouldn't listen. But she found that she was listening, that she couldn't stop listening. She still didn't feel like eating, but the soup smelled heavenly, just as Mona said, and the smell, for now, was enough.

"We did walk in the mountains. That's what I remember most. Walking, walking, walking. We carried our belongings, hid for a time, slept a little, and then walked some more. We did walk barefoot in the snow for two weeks. But I never got frostbite. The walking kept my feet warm, and when I lay down I wrapped my feet in dry clothing. That was the secret—dry feet. Then one day I got lucky. I found boots on a dead German soldier."

"You didn't kill him?" Mona asked casually, as if asking if there were carrots in the soup.

"No." Mutti smiled. "He did get shot by somebody else. I took only his boots, not his life."

Mona laughed as if that was the funniest joke. Carrie thought that Mrs. Brockner had a witty side, too—didn't she? It seemed odd, to see Mona so delighted here, and so scowly in the Brockner home. Carrie realized she was a little scowly herself, but Mona and Mutti were too caught up in each other to notice.

"We stayed at a farmhouse for one year. Primitive. Rooftop toilet—you went through a hole in the roof." No fuzzy lid covers, Carrie thought. "We had only a basket of eggs to eat for a month. In the winter we did sleep twelve people pressed together, or we would have frozen to death. In the spring, we worked in the fields. So help me, there were air attacks all the time. We did learn two words in Serbian. If somebody did yell *'cruze'*—circling—you had to hide in the bushes right away. That meant attack planes that circled and did shoot at you. When you heard *'pokrat,'* that meant move, get all your things and go—Germans were coming. We hid in the woods then. That did happen two or three times. We got a terrible fungus that gave us itchy, open sores. Lice did live in those sores. We had fleas. Bedbugs. Everything that could suck your blood, we had." Mutti smiled apologetically. "Not conversation for the table!"

"I don't mind," Mona said, though Carrie was glad she wasn't eating.

But it was from there, in March 1945, Mutti said, that they were truly rescued, transported on a war ship to Bari, Italy, to a displaced persons' camp—Transit Camp No. 1. "Our closes got burned." Did Mona need that translated? No, she didn't. "We took petroleum showers. We did stay in barracks, open-air

128

rooms. We had regular meals—Spam and corned beef. The best! We had two things to do—get in touch with Liesl, Carrie's mother, and get to America."

Mutti's blue eyes got wet. "We wrote to Angus Fraser, who took care of Liesl during the war, and he wrote to Liesl . . . and she came to us. To see her again, after six years of separation—I can't tell you. I left her when she was a girl of thirteen. Now she was nineteen. A young woman."

Carrie was afraid Mutti would dissolve into tears, but before that could happen, Mona got up, gathered up some dishes, and said, "Thank you for the delicious soup."

"Carrie didn't eat a bite!"

"I'm sure she'll have some later. It's too good. Mutti, thank you for talking to me."

After Mona cleared the table, Mutti and Mona hugged each other. It wasn't how Mrs. Brockner always grabbed and hugged Carrie. Somehow this was a real . . . embrace.

Carrie got back into bed and Mona sat on the edge.

Mona took a deep breath and let it out slowly. "I was nine when it happened. The same age as you when your mother died."

"When what happened?"

"I don't know what you'd call it. My 'bad episode,' I guess."

But Carrie never thought of Mona as having bad episodes. Mona was just the way she was, not because of a bad episode or anything else.

"I wanted to run away. I almost took a Greyhound bus. I

counted my money, called the Port Authority, and asked how far away thirty-two dollars would take me."

"I bet whoever you talked to got all suspicious and called the police." Carrie felt nervous. What could make Mona want to run away from a home like hers?

"No, they didn't care. Cleveland, they said. Carrie, I came this close to doing it." She held her thumb and index finger a speck apart. "I thought about it every minute. I had a whole fantasy about Cleveland, the way other people imagine Paris. I used to sit on busses with my mother and think, the woman beside me is a stranger and this bus is going to Cleveland."

"Mona, what happened?"

"Grandma Rosie, that's what happened."

Wait a minute, Carrie almost said out loud. Grandma Rosie doesn't matter. You just push her aside, like something on your plate you don't want to eat.

"My best friend Kay had just moved and I was really lonely."

"I didn't know you had a best friend named Kay."

"Well, I did. Grandma Rosie had been living with us for a year. My uncle in California had already kicked her out and my other uncle in Florida wouldn't even let her in. Grandma Rosie made me cry every single day. She told me I'd never have any more friends, that other kids talked about me behind my back. She said people could tell just by looking at me what I was thinking, and that I had ugly thoughts, and I should be very careful what I said because people had minds like tape recorders and remembered everything."

"Mona, that's so awful! But you didn't believe her."

"Of course I believed her! I was nine years old! I was too

scared to even try to make friends—they could read my ugly thoughts."

"What about your parents? Did they know?"

"They knew and didn't know."

Yes and no—like one of Mutti's answers.

"My mother thought it was maybe my fault, that I was mean to Grandma Rosie or way too sensitive. My father agreed. They didn't think, or didn't want to think, that Grandma Rosie was really crazy. There was a lot of stress in the house, you can imagine." Carrie wondered why in fact Grandma Rosie wasn't right in the head. Carrie's grandfather had been beaten by Nazis. What had happened to Grandma Rosie? "Then my mother put Grandma Rosie in a nursing home upstate. Carrie, everything changed instantly. My parents were a million times less tense and I started making friends again."

Carrie wanted the story to end right there—a happy ending. Downstairs, the doorbell rang. Trick-or-treaters. Carrie heard little kids laughing.

"It lasted about three months. We visited Grandma Rosie every couple of weeks, and with each visit she got more frantic. She cried. She begged to come home. She got eczema, she said, because she was so upset. One night, my parents sat me down on the couch. 'Now this is a family decision,' my mother told me. 'Dad and I think Grandma Rosie should come home, but we all must agree or she stays where she is. Mona, it's up to you.' I couldn't believe it! She was making *me* decide. I couldn't say what I really wanted to say, what I almost did say—no, leave Grandma Rosie where she is, let her rot, for all I care. Then Grandma Rosie would have been right about me. I had ugly thoughts, thoughts that would be remembered forever. So I said what they wanted me to say. 'If she wants to come home, let her come home.'"

It sounded like a bad dream you couldn't wake up from. "So, okay, Grandma Rosie came home."

"Not right away. The next day was even worse. My mother made an appointment for me—with a doctor, she said. She didn't say 'psychiatrist,' but I knew it. Lots of my mother's friends are psychiatrists. This one had very pale, chalky-white skin and bright red hair. I remember thinking, why has my mother brought me to a clown? 'Your mother is thinking of having your grandmother come home,' she said. 'But she made a sacred promise to me that if it would cause you terrible problems, your grandmother would stay upstate. Mona, should she come home or not?' She stared at me, hard. She was some kind of expert on child liars, I guess. 'It's fine,' I told her. She said, 'You're sure? Absolutely, one hundred percent sure? You mean that from your heart of hearts, Mona?' I told her yes, absolutely, one hundred percent, in my heart of hearts. I didn't even know what that meant. I still don't. I wanted to yell at her, do your job! Expose me! Tell my mother you know this child is lying! But she couldn't read my ugly thoughts, Carrie."

Mona was an actress, even back then. She'd fooled a psychiatrist. "It wasn't fair, Mona. It wasn't up to you. You were just a kid." Carrie had always thought, in a weird way, that Liesl was a bad mother—because she died. But Liesl couldn't help dying. Mrs. Brockner actually *chose* to do what she did. And Mr. Brockner did nothing. Carrie thought of Mutti, how Mutti had spent her whole life doing the opposite of nothing.

"Grandma Rosie came home," Mona said. "I stayed away from her, as much as I could. So did my parents. They sort of pretended that even though Grandma Rosie was there, she wasn't really there. They barely spoke to her or looked at her. Like a dance—Ring-Around-Grandma-Rosie."

What Mona was saying about the Brockner home—there was dark in the light. And here, in Mutti's house, there was light in the dark.

"I hate my mother, Carrie."

"I know. I know you do, Mona." Something got rearranged inside Carrie then. She saw Mrs. Brockner as somebody in a magazine—a parent of a runaway. The runaway was Mona, though she'd never left home. *We love you, call collect.*

If Carrie got asked back to the Brockner house, she would be—polite, nothing more, just for show, like Mrs. Brockner's food. She remembered suddenly, vividly, a phrase her mother used to say, and it summed up how she felt—"the bloom is off the rose." Carrie even heard the words in her head in the softly musical tone so natural to her mother, as clearly as if her mother were right there in the room, standing by the window.

Reunion

Chapter 16

Before Carrie even saw Angus Fraser, she heard his loud voice. Her hand shook as she put her key in the lock. *Am I dreaming?*

There was her father, and Mutti—who must've left work extra early—and Angus Fraser. *That man is supposed to be Angus Fraser,* she thought. It took several moments to realize that he was the real thing.

He was bigger than she'd imagined (though she hadn't imagined anything). He got up and came toward her—he looked about six feet four, and a heavyweight, definitely. He had blue-gray eyes, round wire-rimmed glasses, a thin fringe of white hair, dimples, and deep laugh lines.

"Carrie!" he bellowed, hurting her ears. He stood before her, massive in a wool fisherman's sweater and wide-wale tan corduroy pants. He didn't kiss Carrie; instead, he gave her a hug, wrapping her up like a blanket. "Hullo," he said. "Lovely to see you again. You were such a wee thing last time." She didn't want to think about "last time" and "this time." Instead, she thought about his soft, lilting Scottish accent. Amazingly, he sounded like Carrie's mother—the accent Carrie could never place was Scottish. Why hadn't she thought of it before? This man had taught her mother English.

Carrie had on a new blue velour top Mutti had bought her—for this occasion, she supposed. She couldn't say anything to Angus Fraser. She could barely look at him.

Carrie's father, tall and thin with dark circles beneath his eyes, also gave her a hug (and a kiss, too, which felt as light and fluttery as a butterfly) and said, "Come sit, Carrie. Angus has been telling us about his flight."

Angus took up so much air and space that his section of the couch sagged. Carrie sat opposite him.

"Oh, I could have knocked him out!" Angus said. "I had a fight with someone who took my luggage in the baggage claim. He said it was a mix-up—oh, I didn't believe him! Look at my bag—it's one of a kind!" It was a large black leather bag. "A security guard had to hold me back!"

"Maybe it was a mistake," Carrie said tentatively.

"Well, if so, he'll never make it again, I promise you."

Angus talked about all the near-fights he'd had—on ships, in pubs. Carrie wondered whether her father should give him a nickname and promote him. *The Flying-off-the-Handle Scotsman*.

Later, setting the dining room table gave her something to do. Carrie had never eaten there before—a long wooden table with six chairs. First she set two places. But that didn't seem right. Then she remembered that she needed four.

At dinner, after the chicken soup and during the pot roast, Angus talked about haggis, a Scottish dish made with the stomach of a sheep. At one point he interrupted himself. "Carrie, you remind me of Liesl."

Carrie almost dropped her fork. "What?"

"You remind me of your mother. I remember her so well."

"I don't remember you," Carrie blurted out—and could have kicked herself. She was as bad as Grandma Rosie! "I mean, I guess I was too little."

"You were just a wee thing."

"Anyway, my mother was beautiful." She was in this conversation despite herself.

"Yes, she was, but not to herself! I'd tell her she was a lovely lass, and she'd say, 'I'm not beautiful. Helga was beautiful.'"

"I remember Helga," Mutti said. "She was in Liesl's section in the *gymnasium*. More—how do you say it? Classical. A classical beauty."

"Classic," Carrie corrected her.

"Just before things got very bad," Mutti said, "some Austrian officials did go to Liesl's class, to photograph what they called 'the perfect Aryan child' for a German magazine. They right away noticed Helga—who wouldn't? She had thick blonde braids like ropes, and cheeks like apples, and alert blue eyes. They took dozens of pictures—Helga at her desk, Helga reading, Helga in the yard. Only then did they find out—Helga was Jewish. They got real good furious! They took all the rolls of film to the yard and set them on fire. The other children stood at the window, excited by the fire, laughing and shouting. Helga just stared, watching her pictures burn."

"Did she die in the war?" Carrie asked, somehow knowing the answer.

"Very likely so," Mutti replied.

Angus had his own "beautiful girl" story. In his tiny village of

Banchory, near Aberdeen, a hunchback got the most beautiful girl in all of Scotland to marry him: "He told her that before both of them were born, when they were still two souls up in heaven, God planned to make her the hunchback. But he pleaded with God, and convinced God to let him take the hunchback for her, because he loved her that much."

All this talk of beautiful thin girls, even those who died, suddenly made Carrie hungry again. *Hunger hurts,* Mutti had said. It hurts me, too, Carrie thought. And then felt awful. How could she compare herself, overweight and living in safe Belle Heights, to Mutti, who had been imprisoned in nine concentration camps and starved down to eighty pounds? No question about it, she felt about as far from "miraculously pleasant" as it was possible to get. She broke off a piece of bread and chewed it—real Vienna bread, crust hard as a rock, that one of Mutti's customers had baked for her that morning.

"Carrie, you want more chicken water?" Mutti asked.

"Chicken *soup,*" Carrie said, appalled.

Mutti just laughed. "Soup, of course. Sometimes I have trouble with language. Carrie needs to tell me the right way."

"Nonsense!" Angus said. "You speak beautifully, Hilde. You have a charming accent."

"You say charming because you don't want to say ugly!"

Everyone, except Carrie, laughed. Why was that funny? They all laughed, too, at a joke of her father's. Something Liesl had told him, about two foolish German counts sitting opposite each other in a train compartment. One said to the other, "Trade places with me. I'm tired of looking at your face all afternoon."

Carrie felt like she was trying to feel at home in a place where she barely knew the language.

Mutti told a story about the most famous opera singer in Vienna at the turn of the century, Leo Slezak. During *Lohengrin,* Slezak was supposed to glide offstage, singing his heart out, on the back of a prop swan. But he missed his cue—and the swan went off without him. Slezak calmly asked the audience, "What time does the next swan go by?"

Everyone, except Carrie, laughed again.

"Yes." Angus Fraser smiled his big Cheshire Cat smile at Carrie. "You do remind me of Liesl."

Carrie figured he must be out of his mind.

"I have exciting news," Mutti said. "A *Daily News* reporter is coming tomorrow."

"What?" Carrie felt like she was in an elevator with its cables cut. "A reporter is coming *here?*"

"Your father called and got them interested."

"But—why?" Carrie looked at her father accusingly.

He shrugged. "It's a great story. Angus Fraser saved your mother's life, Carrie. He's written letters to her and her family all these years. And now he's come to see us."

"What a big fuss," Carrie said. "Why does it have to be in the newspaper? Why do you have to promote it like it was one of your fighters?"

Now Mutti got firm. "Carrie, you don't have to talk when the reporter comes. You don't have to be in a picture when the photographer takes pictures."

"Pictures, too?" The elevator was plunging through the sub-basement.

"But I expect you to be here and listen."

Carrie nodded. Why was it so bad for a reporter to write a story about Angus Fraser, or a photographer to take his picture with her family? What was wrong with her, anyway?

In the middle of the night, Carrie heard voices downstairs. Silently she made her way out of her room and started down the steps. And then she saw them. Her father—who was supposed to be on a foldout bed in the basement—and Angus, sitting on the couch made up like a bed. Talking. What had happened to her father's dark cloud of silence? Why had it become a cloud-burst of talk?

Carrie listened. Finally, she went back to her room and kept her door open. But the voices kept on, and she went to sleep like that, listening and waiting.

Chapter 17

Carrie woke up to Angus Fraser complaining about his back. "It hurts here, in the lower part," he was telling Mutti.

"You must sleep on a bed tonight," Mutti said.

"Oh, no! I wouldn't dream of it."

This went on for several more minutes. Mutti ordering Angus to trade places with her, or with Ray downstairs, or even with Carrie in her room. But Angus Fraser kept refusing. So stubborn!

Carrie drank some Instant Breakfast—but it wasn't enough for her, so she grabbed some of the bread from last night. When Angus Fraser tried to talk to her, she said she was in a hurry to get to school, and ended up arriving twenty minutes early.

At lunch—which turned out to be rubbery ravioli, testing even Carrie's extraordinary tolerance for cafeteria food—Mona got all excited about the *Daily News*. "You're not going to put on my mother's old sweater, I hope," Mona said. "Where is it, anyway?"

"The laundry."

"So what will you wear?"

Carrie couldn't believe Mona was talking about clothes. "Nothing," she said.

"I don't think they'll print that."

"I meant, nothing special."

"Carrie, I was kidding." Mona squinted at her. "Your hair's different again. The way it used to be. It looks good."

"Anyway, I won't be in any pictures and I'm not talking to any reporter. If you're so interested, you can come and see it for yourself."

"This is really a family thing. Your family."

"But Angus Fraser isn't part of my family."

"Carrie, how can you say that?"

She was upstairs in her room when the reporter and photographer arrived.

"Carrie, come downstairs!" Mutti called.

She'd put on the blue velour top, after all. She didn't know why.

The reporter looked young—he could have been a teenager. Tall, thin, black, with curly hair and light brown eyes like coffee with lots of milk. He wore blue jeans and an Icelandic wool sweater. The photographer was a young woman with close-cropped black hair; she held what looked to Carrie like an extra large floor lamp. Right away she introduced herself as Kim, and said, "I do the family stuff. You got a plug or something I can use? This is my kind of story. The family stuff. Where's the plug?"

Mutti showed her an outlet. Kim needed to turn on the lamp, which was actually a spotlight. For the first time ever, Mutti's living room was flooded with light. The walls, Carrie could see, weren't beige but very pale yellow.

"Chip Anderson," the reporter said, as he shook everyone's hand. When it was Carrie's turn, she didn't say anything. Maybe he'd think she was a mute and leave her alone.

Carrie's father had put on a white button-down shirt and dark brown trousers, and Mutti wore something yellow and silky. Angus Fraser had put on a bright red sweater—not Brockner Red, but close. Anyway, Carrie thought, the paper's in black and white. The living room couches were couches again, no sign of sheets or blankets.

Mutti gave everyone mugs of hot tea and there were some butter cookies on a tray on the coffee table. Liesl's picture was there, too. Everyone sat. Carrie was sandwiched between Mutti and her father on one couch; Angus Fraser and Chip Anderson sat on the other. Kim fooled around with the lighting.

"Will you tell us before you take a picture?" Carrie couldn't help asking her. So much for being a mute!

Kim assured her she would. "I won't be taking any pictures until after Chip finishes up his questions. We always work that way, so we don't step on each other's toes." She smiled at Carrie, who didn't smile back. Carrie didn't want to like anything about the *Daily News*.

Chip Anderson fished a long, thin notebook out of his pocket and asked Angus Fraser his first question: "What kind of work do you do?"

"I'm a beekeeper. A honey farmer, it's called in Scotland. My parents were always so deathly ashamed of me—the 'ne'er do well.' They wanted me to be a doctor. I wouldn't hear of it."

It hardly surprised Carrie that Angus Fraser didn't listen to his parents. Here, he wouldn't even do a simple thing like switch beds. In spite of herself, she found it fascinating that her family's hero was his own family's failure.

"I was tremendously rebellious. As a teenager I ran away from home and became a sailor. My parents said, what a waste. But my motto is, 'Be someone on whom nothing is lost.' I wound up in China."

Stop the presses, Carrie almost said. Angus Fraser was a missing girl! Except that he was a boy.

"Funny, I was such a world traveler, but I was a little nervous to come here to the States! Not as young as I used to be, I suppose."

Strange again, hearing Angus Fraser say he was nervous about this visit, too.

"In China I met a girl from Glasgow, one of the biggest cities in Scotland. I believed in fate—still do—and knew that I was destined to marry this girl. And I did." Carrie could see Chip edge back, away from Angus, who tended to lean in too close. Carrie herself was so close to Mutti, their arms touched. Mutti smelled like soap, nice and clean. "I married Flo and we had a beautiful baby girl, Beatrice. Flo, I'm sorry to say, died many years ago." Carrie wondered if that was why Angus and her father had spoken late into the night. Widowers, comparing notes. "Bea's a grown woman now, married, living in Glasgow, three boys."

"Back in nineteen-thirty-nine, why did you take in a child?" Chip asked.

Angus Fraser shrugged. "It was wartime. It needed to be done. I didn't really give it much thought." He reached for a butter cookie. Carrie was doing the same thing at the same moment and their hands collided. She pulled back quickly. "My wife and I dealt with an international relief organization. They'd put together books of photographs." Angus tapped the picture frame. "In her picture—and this is the same one—Liesl Altmann looked so lost. I felt I was meant to take her home."

Carrie had never imagined her mother as "lost." But when she looked at the picture, she saw he was right. That was her exact expression.

"My farmhouse is two hundred years old, built of pink and gray granite with mica chips. It sparkles like diamonds in the light."

Carrie could practically see the farmhouse, gleaming.

"Liesl must have been very happy there," Chip said.

"Lord, no!" Angus's laughter filled the room. "She couldn't bear it, at first. Wouldn't smile, wouldn't eat, wouldn't talk—well, at first she didn't know the language, of course. All she did was look at her watch. I wondered if she was counting the hours, the minutes, until she could see her parents again. We told her she was lucky to be safe in Scotland, here with us, but I don't think she ever felt lucky or safe. She was a bit of a sad sack, that one."

Wait a minute. Carrie's mother—a sad sack? But she made the ten-year-old twins laugh! She was strong, and confident, and full of adventure. . . . "Mutti," Carrie whispered. "My mother was happy—wasn't she?"

"Not so always," Mutti whispered back.

Angus said, "My bees feed on thousands of tiny blue flowers that grow only on my hillside and nowhere else in the world. It's these flowers that give my honey its special flavor. I got Liesl to taste a teaspoon. That finally got her eating again. I've brought a jar of honey with me. Meadow honey, it's called. Would you like to try it?"

One by one, everyone tasted Angus's honey—taking teaspoons, like cough syrup. Carrie heard praise all around her: "It's heaven!" "The best honey I've ever had." "Soothing inside, like how you wish medicine would taste."

Carrie had a spoonful, too. Would it work its magic on her, as it had for her mother? It was good. Very good, actually. But that was all.

"Gradually Liesl began to notice the hills, the river, the changes in the light. I took it as a personal victory when after several months she stopped wearing the watch altogether. I taught her to read English with 'Dick and Jane' books."

Carrie remembered those from when she was six. Funny, to think of her mother, a big strapping girl of thirteen, sounding out the simple words.

"She helped me with the bees—she became a regular honey farmer! There was only one day she got stung, but seven bees got her that time. She gathered freshly laid eggs, and said she never got used to the chickens on the nest pecking at her. She thought chickens were stupid. She liked our cow, Sheila. Liesl loved milking Sheila. She'd put her cheek right up against Sheila's belly because it was so soft and warm. Sheila liked it, too. But Liesl still had those black moods. Sometimes she stayed in bed all day. My wife and I didn't know what to do."

Carrie couldn't wrap her mind around this. *Liesl sounds like . . . me.*

"When Beatrice was born, she helped out with the baby. I'm

not sure Liesl liked children much, but after three years with us she grew rather attached to our little Bea."

"She didn't like children much?" Carrie said. It was a strange thing to hear about your own mother.

"Oh, she liked you plenty," Angus said easily. "She told me so in her letters."

"She must have been terribly homesick," Chip said.

"It was more than that," Carrie broke in. "I know exactly how she felt. *I'm not supposed to be here.* That was it. *This isn't supposed to be happening.*"

Chip looked at her, swinging around like a spotlight. "Liesl's daughter," he said.

Carrie started to feel . . . bus sick, was how it occurred to her.

"Is it thrilling for you, seeing Angus Fraser?" Chip asked.

Carrie couldn't say anything. She couldn't look at him.

"Carrie's a little shy," Mutti said. "She's thirteen. She goes to Belle Heights Junior High."

Carrie glanced up to see Chip smile and nod. She felt relieved, so relieved—it washed over her like a giant, gentle wave. She wasn't the story here and Chip knew it.

Chip talked to her father while Carrie helped clear away the cookies and mugs of tea. When she'd finished washing the dishes, she came back to the living room to hear Chip say, "I've got all I need. Thank you all—for being part of such a great American story." And he winked at Carrie.

But Carrie had never thought of herself as part of anything, let alone a great American story.

Kim began taking pictures. She didn't even ask Carrie to sit for one. She wanted a shot of Angus entering the house; he had to go out and come in half a dozen times. She wanted Angus and Mutti at the kitchen table, spooning Angus's honey into tea. Carrie stood watching, listening to the clicks of the camera.

Am I dreaming? Carrie asked herself, though of course this wasn't one of her waking signs. *No, I'm awake.* But that wasn't right. *No, I'm half-awake.* That was closer to it. *No, I'm not awake at all.* That was closer still.

I'm not the story here. Click. There was Angus, giving a bear hug to Mutti, who looked radiant, smiling.

Am I dreaming? Yes and no. Mutti's answer felt like the right one.

Click. Her father pumped Angus's hand and grinned. Carrie remembered their voices from the night before.

I'm not the story here.

Suddenly Carrie didn't feel so relieved anymore. How come I'm not the story here? she wondered. I'm not even the story in my own life. I'm missing. *I'm a missing girl.* The sound finally caught up with the echo.

Click. Kim took a picture of a picture—Liesl on the coffee table.

And at that moment Carrie knew why she'd gotten so interested in dreams, in being awake inside dreams. And she thought *Mutti* got things backward! Carrie had to know she was awake while asleep, so she could know she was awake while awake.

Carrie needed dreams to wake up.

Chapter 18

The next few days felt more real than real. Like in some bizarre commercial, colors were brighter, edges sharper, sounds clearer. Dark branches stood out against the sky; the air felt cool on Carrie's cheeks; and she heard, to her surprise, some sparrows in a tree behind Mutti's house. Had they always been there? Belle Heights, with its ordinary houses and lawns, and its extraordinary terminal moraine, felt as if it might become a real place you could actually find on a map.

Mona came over and met Angus Fraser; they were as enchanted with each other as if Angus had been Mrs. Brockner's savior. Later, Mona called Carrie to tell her, "What a great guy he is!"

"Everybody likes Angus," Carrie said softly.

"I'm talking about your father."

"What? He talked to you? He opened his mouth and said words?"

"This was when you were in the basement with the laundry. Honestly, Carrie, if I didn't know any better, I'd think you were back in my house, slaving away on one of my mother's lists."

Carrie liked doing chores now. It was kind of a legacy from the Brockners. "Mona, what did my father say to you?"

"He told me about one of his fighters, a guy who was a child actor and did TV commercials . . . well, you probably know the whole story."

No, she didn't. She didn't know the half of it—or the quarter, or any fraction at all.

At night, every night, she heard her father and Angus talking, sometimes laughing. Occasionally she heard silence, but she knew they were still together, because always the talking started up again. When did they ever sleep?

Chip Anderson's article came out on Saturday, and Carrie's father ran out to get a dozen papers so Angus could take some home.

Carrie clipped a copy for herself, cutting it slowly, carefully, as if it were a blue letter. It was only one column, though it covered the whole length of the page. Next to it were advertisements for Kips—sheets and pillowcases, and intricate embroidered sweaters that caught her eye. Over the column was only one picture—Angus hugging Mutti. But it didn't look staged at all. You could almost feel that warm, strong hug.

FAMILY OF REFUGEE HAS JOYFUL VISIT WITH WW II BENEFACTOR

By Charles Anderson

Many years ago, a desperate mother sent her thirteen-year-old daughter to an unknown place, an unknown future. The girl didn't know anyone in her new home; she didn't even know the language. She was a war orphan from Vienna, fleeing Hitler and certain deportation to a German concentration camp. For months at a time the girl didn't know whether her own real parents had perished.

A kindly man from another land took care of her for three years and kept her safe from the ravages of war. This week in Belle Heights, Queens, that man, a Scotsman, had a joyful visit with the girl's family—the family that now feels like his own.

The girl's mother, Hilde Altmann of Belle Heights, a familiar face to patrons of Luncheonette on Belle Boulevard, recalled seeing her daughter, Liesl, off on the train in 1939. "She wore a green hat," Mrs. Altmann said. "Her red hair looked so beautiful."

The kindly man—Angus Fraser, a honey farmer who lives near Aberdeen—had chosen Liesl's picture from a book of hundreds of pictures of war orphans. The first time Mr. Fraser saw Liesl, getting off the train in Edinburgh, he said, "She looked so frightened with a ticket hanging from her lapel. Right away my wife and I knew we had done a good thing."

Mr. Fraser's wife, Florence, also had red hair, and Liesl was often mistaken for their actual daughter. "But I took care to tell people Liesl was staying with us during the war, and that her real parents were alive," Mr. Fraser said. "Liesl came to church with us, and our minister tried to convert her. But I told him Liesl came to us as Jewish and would remain so, until she was old enough to decide for herself."

After Liesl left Mr. Fraser's farm, she went first to London to work in a boot factory, and then to Germany to work for the Americans, interpreting captured Nazi documents. She was reunited with her parents at a displaced persons' camp in Italy in 1945.

Liesl came to America in 1948 as a war bride—engaged to two men. "In case one changed his mind," Mrs. Altmann explained. While staying with her parents in Brooklyn, Liesl ran into Ray Schmidt, whom she had met in Germany. Mr. Schmidt, who now works as a boxing promoter, got her to break both engagements and marry him. They had a daughter, Carrie, now in eighth grade at Belle Heights Junior High. When Carrie was only five, Angus Fraser came to visit for the first time. Four years later Liesl died after a long illness.

"If Carrie ever wants to visit my home," Mr. Fraser said, "she is most welcome, for as long as she wants to stay."

Mona called to say she loved the story. "Very romantic! I didn't know your mother was engaged to two men at the same time."

"Somebody must've said that to Chip while I was cleaning up."

"I showed it to my mother, don't ask me why," Mona said scornfully. "She skimmed it, and then told me not to leave newspaper on the couch—it leaves smudges. Hey, Carrie, let's go to Scotland and become honey farmers."

"What happened to the old green house?"

"I like this idea better."

But Carrie was only just now getting used to Belle Heights. She looked at the article again—in print, in public, for all the world to see, Angus Fraser was telling her, *My home is your home.* She might do something with that for Mrs. Mendoza, a project about how you could have more than one home. "Scotland—My Other Home." *I've never even been there,* she could begin, *but it was my mother's other home, a long time ago. And it could feel like home to me, too, even if I never go there.*

The phone rang again, right away, so Carrie figured it was Mona calling back, having forgotten to tell her something.

But it was June.

"Hi, remember me?" June spoke in a small voice.

"Of course I remember you. It wasn't so long ago. Also I see you in homeroom every day—"

"I saw the article. Carrie, it was beautiful, it almost made me cry. Your family got in the paper! Your family made history! I remember that story you told about your grandmother. I know Luncheonette. I've eaten there. Oh, my God. I nearly cried." She paused. "Carrie, I did cry."

"That's nice of you to say, June."

"Anyway, I wanted to ask you . . . how's Mona?"

"She's fine."

"Maybe we could all hang out sometime, talk about dreams some more?"

Carrie could hear how nervous she was. "Sure. We could have lunch at Luncheonette—how's that sound?"

"Sounds great! And you can come to my house, too."

Carrie would like that. Not fall madly in love with June's house and memorize it and want to live there forever. Just plain visit.

"You know, when I was at your place, I didn't mean to refuse your food like it wasn't good enough, or something. I eat anything. Except food that turns my mouth a different color. Blueberry pie, things like that. But when I was friends with Regina, I kind of let her boss me around—"

"You guys aren't friends anymore?"

"She and Ruby Stevens. They're thick as thieves."

"Thick as what? I never heard of that."

They talked for so long, Mutti had to get them off the phone so she could call a cab to take Angus Fraser to the airport.

Carrie watched Angus Fraser pack his black leather bag. The couches were back in two pieces; the shelves were empty. But even once all the books got put back, without Angus the place, Carrie realized, would still feel empty. Mutti and her father were talking and drinking tea with honey in the kitchen.

"I came to say good-bye," Carrie said. "Or maybe I should say hello first, since I never did say it." But this didn't feel like *hello* or *good-bye*. More like an odd kind of reunion.

Angus grinned. "I have a good-bye present for you. Or a hello present, if you prefer."

He handed her a half dozen photographs. It felt like getting a dream gift from a dream friend. "I didn't show these to Chip or Kim, when they were here, or to your father or Hilde. I wanted you to have them."

Carrie knew, even before looking at them, that she wanted to put these pictures and the article in an album of their own. But it might look so empty. Well, she could add her own pictures to it—for the rest of her life.

The first one, in full color, showed a freckled boy with hair the color of carrots, standing in front of a farmhouse that sparkled like diamonds.

"That's one of my grandsons, Andrew."

The next one was in black-and-white—a dark-haired woman in a wheelchair, outside the farmhouse, her hair wild in the wind, her jacket flapping.

"That's Flo, after the stroke. About a year before she died."

"Is it always so windy on the farm?"

"Always. We're on top of a hill. Look, here's one with your mother and Beatrice."

All the other pictures were also black-and-white. In the first, Liesl wore a heavy flannel shirt, and her hair was blown across her face. She was holding up a baby by the wrists. The baby looked afraid she might fall.

"This next one is the view from your mother's window on the second floor."

Carrie saw gentle hills, scattered trees, Sheila the cow, and great clusters of tiny, delicate flowers—the kind that might sing in a fairy tale.

"And there's me, quite some time ago!"

Angus Fraser was a young man, slim and handsome, life shining in his eyes.

She turned to the last picture. "Wait a minute—where'd you get this?" Had Mutti somehow given him a picture of Carrie at the kitchen table?

"What do you mean?"

"Did Mutti send this to you?"

"Carrie—it's a picture of your mother in Scotland, sitting at our kitchen table. She's leaning forward, her hair's a wee bit wild, the kitchen's a wee bit dark. Always dark in that room."

She couldn't believe it. Liesl looked exactly like her—without looking like her at all. "She wasn't very happy, was she?"

"She had a hard time, being lucky and safe when her parents weren't."

"I sort of know the feeling." Carrie spoke so softly she wasn't sure Angus caught it. She heard a car pull up to the curb, and a door slam. Angus's taxi.

"Good-bye, my dear," Angus said.

"But—I don't have anything for you!" She could have kicked herself. She should have gotten him a going-away present.

"Of course not. I don't want anything or need anything—nor did I expect anything."

"But I wanted to—I don't know. Or maybe I do know." The cab driver would have knocked by now. She spoke during the time when there was no time, saying things she hadn't even said to herself. "You saved my mother's life, and I was all that was left of a good deed. It wasn't that I didn't want to see you. I didn't want you to see me. I mean, I wasn't beautiful, like my mother. I sure wasn't miraculously pleasant. I was so afraid of the *Daily News*—I thought there might be a headline—I could almost see it, SAVIOR OF BEAUTIFUL REFUGEE SHOCKED TO FIND SHORT, FAT, UNGRATEFUL DAUGHTER. I didn't want you to find—a sad ending. I knew you expected a happy ending. To a great American story, like Chip said."

"What I expected was a young American girl in the process of growing up, and that's just what I found. And growing up is wonderful in itself."

"What's so wonderful about it?"

"You get to see what happens next. Isn't that all you could want from a story?"

She shrugged. "I guess so."

"Carrie, you're not a happy ending or a sad ending. You're a story-in-the-middle. That's what it is to be young." He gave her a swift, gentle kiss—right on her dimple. The pendulum was making contact now. And for the first time she remembered what was truly amazing about that Edgar Allan Poe story. The pendulum cut the man's skin, but only on the surface; he'd rubbed food on his restraints so that rats, hundreds of rats, would gnaw through them—and set him free.

Chapter 19

Carrie couldn't sleep. After hours of tying her sheets and blankets into sailor's knots, she went downstairs.

Her father was still up, too, at the kitchen table. He was dressed, and working—writing in pencil on a yellow legal pad. "Did I wake you?" he asked.

"How could you? You're quiet as a mouse."

"I had the light on——"

"I could sleep outside in the sun, if I had to. But I can't sleep now."

He smiled, a little sadly. "I know, Carrie. I miss him, too."

She looked at what he was writing:

Kenny McBurt, called "No Dirt McBurt," is a 29-year-old Long Island bantamweight who teaches boxing to kids. His improving record stands at 21 wins (with 9 KOs) against 17 losses. "Extra Tough" in the ring but "Ever There" to his wife.

"I know that KO means knockout, but I forget how heavy a bantamweight is."

"One hundred and twelve pounds."

"Romantic. The part about his wife, I mean."

"He could win a few more fights—that would be really romantic!" Even in the kitchen light, she could see his dark hair beginning to go gray. He was forty-four now, an age her mother would never get to be.

"Dad, I heard you at night. Talking to Angus."

"Carrie, I'm sorry if we kept you up—"

"You didn't. What were you talking about?"

His face darkened as if a shadow had passed over him. "This and that," he said.

She got up to leave. The shadow, she knew, was the dark cloud of silence.

But he called her back. "Wait. Sit down, Carrie. Angus and I talked about Liesl. It wasn't so easy for me. At least not at first."

She sat down again.

"Angus wanted to hear about how Liesl and I met. I thought he already knew the story. Maybe he did—maybe he felt it was good for me to tell it again. That man could have been a first-rate shrink!"

Carrie agreed. Psychiatrist *or* psychologist. "Dad, I don't know the story. Why don't you tell it to me?" She remembered how surprised Mutti had been, when she'd asked for stories about the war. But her father didn't seem so surprised. Angus had broken the ice—ice as thick as the glacier that formed the terminal moraine.

"Your mother was an officer, a lieutenant in the British Army, supervising seven other girls and processing GIs waiting to go home. I was one of those GIs. As soon as I saw your mother, in her green army uniform and green cap, I fell in love."

Carrie's mother, it seemed, spent her life as a woman in a green hat. *Am I dreaming? No, I'm awake. Wide awake.*

"I couldn't help myself—I started yelling, 'I'm in love! I'm in love!' Everyone in the office laughed. Your mother was so embarrassed."

"She hated scenes, didn't she?" Carrie wasn't sure how she knew that. Some things were memories; some were only echoes of memories.

"Not only that, but I wasn't her type at all! Not too bad-looking, mind you, but not a proper young man from Vienna. I asked her out on a date. She said no. Probably she was engaged—she ended up getting engaged five times! Then I found out from a friend of hers that she loved the opera. So I got some opera tickets—she couldn't resist that! But I fell asleep during the first act; she barely spoke to me on the walk home. That was our first—and only—date."

Angus was right. This was good for her father, Carrie could see it. As good as Angus's honey had been for Liesl in Scotland. "Speaking of dates," she broke in, "are you dating now?" She hadn't known she was even interested.

He shook his head. "I have my work. It's enough—enough for now." He looked at her. "We were so right for each other, Carrie, and you'd never think it, considering the different worlds we came from. It was pure luck. Good luck, for a change."

"Go on," she said.

"I was about to be shipped back home to America, and didn't think I'd ever see your mother again. And I didn't—not for three years. By that time I was engaged myself, and living in

Brooklyn. One day, on my way to my fiancée's house, my car broke down on Pitkin Avenue, and I had to get on the bus. And what happened, three stops later? Your mother and Mutti got on. I couldn't believe it. I still can't believe it. I starting yelling, 'I don't believe it! I don't believe it!' Mutti told Liesl—in German—not to speak to me, that I was a crazy American. I rushed them both off the bus, and took them straight to my mother's house—so she could meet the girl I was going to marry. My mother didn't like Liesl. She told me, that girl is an immigrant."

"Did your mother try to break it up?"

"Oh, sure. But we got married three days later."

Carrie had to take a long, deep breath. They hadn't known each other at all! One disaster of a date and a chance meeting on a bus. "Just think—what if your car hadn't broken down, what if your fiancée lived on a different bus route, what if Mutti and Liesl had taken a later bus?"

"Listen to this." Now he was the father she remembered, eager to tell her things. "During the war one day, your mother finished her shift at the boot factory in London. She waited for the bus that would take her home. Then she realized she'd left her bag at the factory. She headed back, but saw that the bus was coming. At the very last moment she decided to get on the bus and pick up the bag the next day. Several minutes later, from the bus, she heard an explosion. The whole factory was gone, blown up. What if she'd gone back for the bag? What if the bus had come two minutes later? What if there'd been something so valuable in the bag she'd gone back, anyway? You see how it was, Carrie?"

"Yes." If any one of those things, or dozens of others, hadn't happened exactly as they did, Carrie Schmidt wouldn't be here. Her life depended on a very specific chain of "what-ifs." Mona's parents had known each other a long time, with lots of friends in common; if they hadn't met at one frat party, they'd have met a week later at the next one. Carrie's parents had had only two unlikely chances to meet. But they'd done it.

It made Carrie feel special. And now she lived in Belle Heights, Bus Capital of the World! She'd never look at busses the same way again. Who knew when, at any moment, a bus could change your life, or save it, or deliver you to your long-lost love, or your best friend forever?

"When Liesl found out her parents were alive, she rushed across Europe. When she saw Papa and Mutti, they were terribly thin and malnourished. She'd snuck into Italy, dressed as an American GI—she didn't have the proper papers. I asked her how she got away with it, and she said, 'Oh, those were silly times.' But it was Papa and Mutti, not Liesl, who wound up with papers to bring them to America—after three years in the displaced persons' camp. A Jewish organization paid their way to cross the Atlantic, and arranged for them to move into an apartment in Brooklyn, a 'cold-water flat.' When Liesl came to America, she had to get married within three weeks or leave. She seemed happy enough about our wedding, though. She barely knew me, Carrie, but she liked me. I cheered her up. I was the only one who could."

Angus had said that, too. Liesl was sad. Carrie was sad, too— *but she wasn't a sad ending.*

"Liesl loved America. She was so proud to become a citizen five years ago. She loved New York City—all of it. Do you remember, Carrie, she took you to the ceremony, and you both went to the Statue of Liberty, and she bought you hot chestnuts? You burned your fingers."

"I don't remember." It haunted her, this forgetting, never knowing when something would come back, clear and intact, or if only a hint of it would emerge, or if it was lost forever, as if it had never even happened.

But then she got an idea. "Dad, can I borrow your tape recorder?"

Chapter 20

After school on Monday Carrie brought her father's tape recorder, big as a briefcase—he never traveled without it—all the way to Luncheonette.

Mutti was in her white apron. "Carrie, what a wonderful surprise!" she said, but it was as if she'd been expecting her. Mutti said she was finishing up—everybody else had gone home early because a blizzard was coming. Light snow was already falling.

Inside, Luncheonette was warm and cheerful, with several enormous stoves, each with half a dozen burners, a long shiny formica counter, high stools, dark red padded booths, leafy hanging plants, and the smell of good food and lots of it.

"Why did you bring that?" Mutti eyed the tape recorder suspiciously as Carrie sat at the counter.

"I want to tape you."

"I don't want to be taped. Two weeks ago I was gamma-rayed at the doctor's."

"*X-rayed,* Mutti."

"I was more dead than alive when I left his office, I can tell you that."

"Taping means you have a conversation. I ask you questions. You give me answers. You talk, I listen, okay?"

"But why tape me?" Mutti bit her lip.

"Because I want to remember things, Mutti. Because I've forgotten so much already." She held the microphone close to Mutti, and turned on the machine. Two large spools of tape rotated slowly, silently. "Please tell me about Yugoslavia."

Mutti didn't say a word.

"Mutti, just talk."

"It was beautiful," Mutti said carefully into the microphone. "Yugoslavia is a most beautiful country."

"Mutti!"

"The mountains were breathtaking." Mutti wrapped her palm over the microphone, and whispered, "It was terrible! We had to climb mountains in the snow. I weighed eighty pounds."

"Tell the machine!"

"Oh, no, I couldn't. It's not nice."

Carrie switched off the tape recorder. "What do you mean, not nice?"

"You don't know who will listen."

"Me—I'll listen. Nobody else. Mutti, you make it sound like a vacation in the Alps."

"I was a hunted animal."

"Tell the tape!"

But Mutti just sat there. She looked at the tape recorder, and back up at Carrie, several times. And Carrie saw that Mutti really couldn't do it. She could trick German soldiers, she could walk barefoot in the snow, she could kill giant screaming rats, but she couldn't speak while spools of tape turned in circles. Even Mutti had her limits.

Carrie turned the recorder off. Traffic rumbled by on Belle Boulevard. Death is like Belle Boulevard, she thought suddenly. A twisty, two-way street. The dead person says good-bye simply by dying, but then you have to say good-bye inside your heart to the dead person. It doesn't just click in by itself, like a streetlight when it gets dark.

"Besides," Mutti said, "I don't talk English so good."

"You speak beautifully."

"Carrie."

"Well, I understand you."

Mutti took out a huge bowl from her side of the counter, emptied an enormous ladle of vegetable soup into it, and pushed it across to Carrie.

"Think I have enough?"

"There's plenty more."

"Mutti, I was kidding!"

"Don't joke about not having enough food, Carrie. When we first came to America, I got a job making sandwiches and coffee for a Viennese bridge club. I never saw food like that, not for years! I got real good fat. But I had to quit that job because everybody spoke only German and I was afraid I'd never learn English. People told me to read newspapers and detective novels. That was how I learned a new language and all about America. I did find out you can't go to Macy's and bargain down prices—the cashiers get mad and call the manager."

Carrie laughed. Too bad she couldn't tape this. She told herself, *One, I will remember, two, I will remember, three, I will remember*—it was worth a try. She tasted the soup. Wonderful. "Did you make this?"

Mutti nodded. "I wanted to own a luncheonette, so we'd never be hungry again. I would stay at the cash register and Liesl would cook. Did she want to be a cook? No! She was very happy working at Saks as a hat model."

"My mother was a model?" Like Veruschka! Carrie could picture her, in one green hat after another.

"Just for a few months. I remember thinking, 'Now all we need is somebody to buy us a luncheonette.' Needless to say, nobody ever did. But when I did see this place—'Luncheonette' in big letters across the sky—I knew I wanted to work here."

"And you work hard."

"Oh, yes. And I enjoy it. I learned this from my father. He did work long hours as an accountant. My mother wasn't able to work—she got excedrin headaches."

"What?"

"How do you say it? Migraines."

"Mutti, Excedrin is a brand of aspirin, not really a kind of headache."

"Oh. That's not how it sounds on television." She took off her apron and sat on a stool beside Carrie. "My mother's headaches were terrible. She had to pull the shades and put out the lights. My little brother and I had to sit there in absolute silence, not one word."

"You have a brother?" Carrie was shocked. Mutti had never mentioned him.

"He was fifteen years younger than me. When he was born, I played with him like a doll. When he was twenty-seven, I got him out of Vienna, on one of three ships heading for Palestine. All three got captured on the Danube, and everybody on board was killed."

There were so many relatives Carrie would never know—so much loss. Suddenly she felt flooded by it. It filled her up, in a way. But how could emptiness fill you up?

"What were your parents' names?"

"Agatha and Joachim. My mother was beautiful, Carrie—but too strict and too vain. She put a wine cork into a flame and used the soot to dye her hair black."

"Not exactly Born Blonde!"

"When she found makeup on me, she did wash my face with milk."

Mutti, Carrie realized, didn't really like her mother. A beautiful mother. Does beauty skip a generation? If Carrie had a daughter, would she be the most beautiful of all?

"That reminds me," Carrie said. "Mom would peel a cucumber, and wash my face with the peel. Not the outside—the inside of the outside. It felt cool and made my skin feel tight. Not because she found any makeup on me, or anything. I was way too young for that. She thought I'd like it—and I did."

Mutti said her father was the nicest man she'd ever known. "He let his mother-in-law live in our house, even though my mother's sisters wouldn't allow her in their own houses. That woman, my grandmother, did go through everyone's closets, pretending to be looking for something. My father just laughed.

'Let her look,' he said. He laughed so much of the time. She lived with us for twenty years."

"Twenty years! I didn't know you lived with your grandmother, too. You and me . . . and Mona."

"My grandmother was not a beauty," Mutti said. "Same as me."

"Same as me, too."

"Just as well."

She could at least have put up an argument!

"You have to worry about beautiful girls. When Liesl was seventeen, an English lord asked her to marry. He had a mansion and was the only child of rich parents."

"Might have been the best thing for her."

"Oh, no, Carrie! He wasn't nice, not at all. Liesl said he yelled at the servants. Besides, Liesl loved your father. And you'd never have been born."

"So what?" Carrie looked down at her soup—she'd eaten all of it—and at her legs, spread out over the stool. "One less fat girl in Queens!"

"You're not fat," Mutti said quietly. "You have good teeth. You'll be pretty enough someday."

Carrie looked up at Mutti. She had the bluest eyes, the sweetest eyes.

"Don't be old and bitter, Carrie. I can be old and bitter. My days are counted."

"Numbered," Carrie corrected her. "But you're not old and bitter. I mean, you're the one who starved, but I eat too much. You suffered, and I'm the one who whines. I feel like Alice through the looking glass. It's all backward."

Just then Mutti turned on the tape recorder and spoke into the microphone. "Don't worry so much, Carrie. You'll figure it out. You and your friend, Mona." And clicked it off.

Which reminded Carrie. She had an errand to run.

The blizzard fizzled out and there was only a dusting of snow. Mona came over for dinner. Carrie set the table in the dining room. Just before they all sat down, Mona said to Carrie, "I have something for you."

"I have something for you, too."

Mona's present was a color picture of Carrie in a sturdy wooden frame—the picture her father had taken. "It came out great," Mona said, "even in that stupid sweater."

"I'm thinking of giving that stupid sweater away. To Regina." Mona laughed.

Carrie looked at the girl in the picture. Her expression was funny. She looked like she wasn't sure whether to smile or not. Carrie placed it next to her mother's picture. Same expression, exactly. There, in the Brockner home, Carrie looked . . . lost.

Dear Diary, she would write later. *It's me—Carrie. No, not Mona! If you want to know what I look like, take a look at the bookshelf downstairs. There are two pictures, me and my mother. Here's how you can tell who is who. She's in black and white. I'm in color. Her picture was carried around for years and is a little frayed. Mine is brand new. She's thin. I'm maybe not so thin. She's beautiful. I'm sort of in the shadow of beautiful. Even so, we're like the South Pole and the North Pole. Alike, and a whole world apart.*

Then Carrie gave Mona her gift—an embroidered sweater

from Kips. Not cashmere, of course, but soft anyway. Blue, with delicate, colorful stitches all around the neck and shoulders. Mona slipped out of her turtleneck and put it on right away. Just as Carrie had imagined, Mona looked stunning in it.

And Mona made herself right at home.

Chapter 21

Carrie was dreaming.

She sat with Mutti at the kitchen table, eating an enormous bowl of vegetable soup. This was in full, brilliant color—Carrie saw orange carrots, sun-yellow corn, beans the color of a freshly cut lawn. But the poison-ivy wallpaper was gone, replaced by grasscloth—and Mona was there, too, eating more heartily than Carrie.

"This soup is heaven!" Mona raved.

Between them on the table, Carrie noticed a three-cent stamp with Mutti's face on it, regal as Mount Rushmore. "Mutti, you're famous!" she cried out. "Your face is on a stamp!"

Mutti shrugged. "I'm not so famous. It's only for three cents."

Mona laughed and gave Carrie a look—You see? You see how wonderful she is? Yes, Carrie could see. She knew, as if she'd known it for some time, that she wanted to live with Mutti from now on, not just for a year. Her father traveled so much, anyway; they could get rid of the apartment in Spruce Hills; she could fix up her room; it was only a matter of details.

Carrie looked at the stamp again. Now it said four cents, and there was Liesl, her face somewhat hidden by her hair blowing wildly, on a Scottish hilltop.

Am I dreaming? Yes, I'm dreaming!

Suddenly Carrie got scared. "If your face is on a stamp, that means you're dead." It felt awful, just saying it out loud. "You're not dead, are you?"

"Not at all," Mutti assured her.

So Carrie felt better. She reached over to hold Mutti's hand, the delicate skin like a blue letter. But the grasp was strong. It occurred to her—here was a perfect opportunity to get a dream gift from a dream friend. "Do you have something for me?"

Mutti seemed ready for this. She licked the stamp—now it was worth two cents, and showed Angus's face with a bee buzzing around him—and stuck it right on Carrie's dimple, where Angus had kissed her. "A stamp of approval," Mutti said.

"That's baby Bea on the stamp," Mona said. "Get it—bee?"

This sounded silly, even for a lucid dream. The stamp fell off, and Carrie gave it back to Mutti.

"See, now you're giving Mutti the stamp of approval," Mona said. "You're telling her, you're proud to be an immigrant's granddaughter—and an all-American girl, too. You can be both." Mona laughed. "It's funny. Angus gave you his two cents, and now he's on a two-cent stamp."

"I'm not sure why that's funny."

"You're supposed to ask some questions, remember?"

It took Carrie a moment. "Who am I?"

"You're a missing girl," Mona responded.

"Who are you?"

"I'm a missing girl, too."

"What do I need to know?"

"We're missing girls, but we found each other."

"But, if we're found, how come we're still missing?"

"You're missing the point." Mona laughed again. "Get it?" No question about it, Mona was laughing more in this dream than in all the time Carrie had known her. "I'm missing out on . . . part of myself. But I'm getting it back, thanks to you. Thanks for the gift, too. I like my green hat."

That didn't sound right. Carrie had given her something, but it wasn't a green hat, was it?

"Between you and Mutti, there's a missing generation. That's some generation gap! Words can be funny in dreams. Your mother was a missing girl, long ago. Now she's missing again because she's not here."

"She's gone—she's really gone. She told me so herself."

"You miss her, don't you?"

"Yes." But she no longer wanted to sleep through the rest of her life. She felt Mutti's strong hand inside her own. Mona smiled like a beautiful old house opening its front door for you.

Carrie opened her eyes. She remembered the dream—maybe not word-for-word, but close enough. She even had a title for it.